"My dear good girl, I take a fatherly interest in the nurses who work for me."

Dr. Everard van Tijlen didn't look in the least fatherly; he looked shockingly handsome, very sure of himself and slightly amused. Charity's tongue spoke the words she had thought but never intended to voice. "You didn't look in the least fatherly the other evening."

Her green eyes sparkled with rising temper, not improved at all by his laugh. "I'm flattered you were sufficiently interested to notice us," he said smoothly, "but I must point out that I said I was fatherly toward my nurses."

She bit savagely into a sandwich. If that wasn't a snub, she would like to know what one was. "I'm not in the least bit interested," she began haughtily.

He was smiling faintly. "A pity..."

Romance readers around the world will be sad to note the passing of **Betty Neels** in June 2001. Her career spanned thirty years, and she continued to write into her ninetieth year. To her millions of fans, Betty epitomized the romance writer, and yet she began writing almost by accident. She had retired from nursing, yet her inquiring mind still sought stimulation. Her new career was born when she heard a lady in her local library bemoaning the lack of good romance novels. Betty's first book, *Sister Peters in Amsterdam,* was published in 1969, and she eventually completed 134 books. Her novels offer a reassuring warmth that was very much a part of her own personality. She was a wonderful writer, and she will be greatly missed. Her spirit will live on in all her stories, including those yet to be published.

THE BEST *of*

BETTY NEELS

THE
GEMEL RING

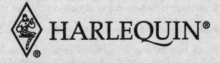

HARLEQUIN®

TORONTO • NEW YORK • LONDON
AMSTERDAM • PARIS • SYDNEY • HAMBURG
STOCKHOLM • ATHENS • TOKYO • MILAN • MADRID
PRAGUE • WARSAW • BUDAPEST • AUCKLAND

ISBN 0-373-51199-X

THE GEMEL RING

Copyright © 1974 by Betty Neels.

This edition published by arrangement with Harlequin Books S.A.

® and TM are trademarks of the publisher. Trademarks indicated with ® are registered in the United States Patent and Trademark Office, the Canadian Trade Marks Office and in other countries.

Visit us at www.eHarlequin.com

Printed in U.S.A.

CHAPTER ONE

THE QUEUE of cars waiting to go aboard the ferry which would take them across the River Schelde to Breskens, so that they might continue their journey to the Dutch border, was large, untidy and impatient, and not the least impatient of the car drivers was Lieutenant-Colonel Dawson, retired, whose somewhat peppery disposition was ill-equipped for delays of any kind. After only a few moments of coming to a halt behind an enormous trans-continental transport, he was already drumming on the wheel with his fingers, poking his head out of the window, and snorting in a rising indignation, actions which caused his wife, sitting in the back of the car with their younger daughter, to murmur soothingly: "Think of your blood pressure, dear," and exchange a wary glance with her companion. Her well-meaning remarks did nothing to help, however her husband began a growling diatribe about foreigners and blew out his military moustache, a sure sign of growing ill-temper—a sign noted by the girl sitting beside him, for she said with an affectionate matter-of-factness: "Don't worry, Father—I'll go and see what the hold-up is—it can't be anything much."

She got out of the car as she spoke and began to make her way towards the head of the queue. She was a tall, well-built girl, her rich, red-brown hair tied back with a silk scarf, her attractive face, with its straight nose and nicely curved, too-big mouth, made almost beautiful by a pair of green eyes, fringed by lashes whose curly length, while genuine, gave rise to a good deal of speculation amongst those who met her for the first time.

She made her way now through the press of cars, intent on finding the cause of the delay, feeling a little guilty about it, for it was at her suggestion that her father had agreed to return across Holland from Bremen, where they had been visiting an old friend, instead of driving down through Germany to Cologne and across to the coast to catch the ferry. It wasn't the first time they had made the trip; each time she had wanted to see more of Holland and each time there had been some reason why they shouldn't. And now she had had her own way and it looked as though it was to result in her fiery parent having a fit of bad temper.

She sighed and caught the admiring glance of a lorry driver as she wormed her way between the cars; he called to her and she answered him readily in his own language in her well-taught boarding-school French. She could see the cause of the delay now— the small group of people crowding round an Opel Rekord, peering in at a man lying back in the driver's seat, while one of the dock police bent over him. Charity sighed again, foreseeing a lengthy delay before they could get on to the ferry; the man, if he were ill, would have to be taken away by ambulance or taxi; his car would have to be moved too, for it was the first in line and was blocking one lane of traffic... She edged her way to the policeman's side and enquired if she could help. "I am a nurse," she explained, and at his blank look repeated the remark in tolerable German.

The man understood her this time and broke into voluble talk, half German, half Dutch—the driver of the car had slumped across the wheel of his car with no warning, he explained, luckily he was at a standstill—no one had noticed at first, not until he had made no move when the barrier was raised for the cars to start going on board the ferry.

Charity nodded as she undid the man's collar and tie and took his pulse. It wasn't too bad, a little rapid, perhaps, and he was very pale. A faint, probably—it was a warm day in late June and even though there was a wind blowing from the sea, it was hot sitting in a car in the sunshine. She leaned across him, tilted his chair back and slipped a cushion behind his head. It wasn't a heart attack, she was sure, nor did he look desperately ill; all the same she asked: "A doctor? There may be one in one of the cars."

The policeman nodded and spoke to someone in the group; he moved away at a rapid trot and Charity asked a little diffidently: "Could you get rid of this crowd?"

They melted away at the policeman's order and she bent over the man again. His pulse had improved, she was counting it when the door on the opposite side of the car was opened and she looked up to encounter the gaze of a very large man whose grey eyes, after the briefest of glances, dropped to the unconscious man between them.

"You're a doctor?" asked Charity, speaking in her stiff, correct German and giving him no time to reply. "His pulse is better and quite strong—his pupils are all right too, though he has a squint…"

"It will be better if we speak English," said the man, with only the faintest trace of an accent. He was opening his bag as he spoke. "You have a very marked English accent, you know."

She would have liked to have made some telling reply to this piece of rudeness; her German was good enough not to have merited it, but she was forced to remain silent because he was using his stethoscope and by the time he had finished examining his patient, the man was showing signs of returning consciousness and presently opened his eyes.

It was apparent when he spoke that he was an American; it was also apparent that he had no idea why he had fainted. In answer to the doctor's few inquiries he admitted to a tingling sensation in his hands. "I felt kinda jerky," he explained. "I guess I've been overdoing it a bit."

To the doctor's suggestion that he should spend the rest of the day at an hotel, have a good night's sleep and continue his journey on the following day, he agreed without enthusiasm, although when the doctor went away to make arrangements to have the car moved and a taxi fetched he raised no objection. His colour was normal again, indeed, he seemed perfectly well again—it must have been the heat, thought Charity, and wondered uneasily about the squint, because the man wasn't squinting any more.

"I'm grateful to you, little lady," he said gallantly, and Charity, a nicely curved five feet ten inches in her stockings, suppressed a giggle. "My name is Arthur C. Boekerchek, from Pennsylvania, USA, I'm at The Hague, attached to the Trades Mission." He gave her a hard stare. "And what's your name, ma'am?"

"Charity Dawson, from England, and if you're sure you're quite all right, I'll be getting back to our car." She put out a hand. "I hope you'll be quite fit after a rest, Mr Boek—Boekerchek. Goodbye."

He shook her hand. "You a nurse?" he wanted to know, and when she nodded: "Which hospital?" She told him, said goodbye for a second time and turned on her heel.

Charity couldn't see the doctor anywhere as she went through the crush of cars and transports. She admitted to herself that she would have liked to have seen him again, if only to tell him that his manners were bad. She wondered which country he came from; his English was faultless, but he wasn't an Englishman. She had almost reached her father's car when she caught sight of him, strolling ahead of her to the back of the queue. Six feet and several inches besides, she guessed, and with the shoulders of an ox. Not so very young either, with that grizzled hair, but very good-looking. His laconic manner had irritated her, and she frowned, remembering it, as her father said: "Well, what on earth was it all about, Cherry?"

She got into the car and explained why she had been so long, making rather less of the doctor than she need have done, so that her mother asked: "Wasn't he a nice man, dear?" and Lucy wanted to know: "And what was he like?"

Charity bit her lip. "I only said about two words to him, Mother, so I couldn't possibly know if he's nice—and I didn't notice what he was like." Which wasn't true.

She saw him again—when they drove off the ferry at last, on the south side of the river and started up the road towards Sluis and Belgium. He passed them, driving a white Lamborghini Espada. He was travelling fast too. Charity pondered the fact that such a placid man as he had appeared to be and not young any more either should own such a powerful car and drive it, moreover, with all the nerve of someone half his age. She kept her surprised thoughts to herself, however, even when her father made some derogatory remark concerning the youth of today driving flash cars they probably couldn't afford.

"They're very expensive," pointed out the Colonel. "Probably some pop singer," he added disgustedly, and Charity, her head bent over the map, wondered what the doctor would have said to that. It was a great pity that she would never know.

She still had a few days of her holiday left; driving down to Budleigh Salterton beside a calmed and rested parent, she was thankful for them. She hadn't really wanted to go to Bremen; she would have preferred to have stayed at home, pottering in the garden and taking the dogs for long walks on the common, but somehow she had found herself agreeing to accompany her parents and sister, mainly because she knew that her calm common sense could cool her father's little rages when her mother or Lucy aggravated them.

He was getting elderly, she thought lovingly, glancing sideways at him as they drove westwards; small things annoyed him, and Lucy, younger by five years than herself, had a gentle nature whose acceptance of his contrariness merely irritated him still further. Her mother, of course, was perfectly able to manage him, but she was recovering from a bout of ill-health and hadn't yet regained her usual fire and spirit. He was a devoted husband and a kind and indulgent father; his irascible nature had never bothered her—it didn't

bother her brother George, either, although now that
he was away from home, he seldom encountered it.

Her thoughts were interrupted by her father's en-
quiry as to where they should stop for lunch and her
mother's "Somewhere quiet, dear," and Lucy's
"We've just passed such a nice hotel," were neither
of them much use. She said peaceably before he could
speak: "How about that place in Petersfield? It's right
on the square and easy to park the car." Even as she
made this sensible suggestion she was wondering
with one tiny corner of her mind where the doctor
was now. She moved restlessly in her seat; it was
strange how he had remained in her thoughts. She told
herself with her usual sense that it was probably because he had annoyed her and had been so very good-
looking.

They arrived home in the early evening and the
next few hours were taken up with fetching Nell and
Bliss, the two English setters, from the kennels, unpacking and helping her mother to get a meal. It was
nice to be home again, back in the unpretentious Ed-
wardian house perched up on the hill behind the little
town, with its large garden and only a glimpse between the trees of the neighbouring houses. Charity
had been born there and been brought up—with suitable intervals at boarding school—in its peace and
comfort. She knew, now that she was older, that there
wasn't a great deal of money, but looking back, she
couldn't remember feeling anything but secure and

well cared for, and although the house was a little bit shabby now, it still provided the same comfort.

She went up to her room, and instead of unpacking, hung out of the window which overlooked the side of the house where her father grew his roses; they were in full bloom now and their scent filled the evening air. For some reason which she couldn't guess at, she sighed, unpacked and went downstairs again to undertake the task of setting the supper table so that Lucy, who was more or less engaged to the doctor's son down the lane, could pay him a quick visit.

The remaining days of Charity's holiday went far too quickly, taken up as they were with the pleasurable occupation of discussing Lucy's still distant wedding, taking her mother to Exeter to shop, exercising the dogs and helping her father sort through the mass of papers he had spent years in collecting, with an eye to writing a book on military strategy during the last war. She thought, privately, that the book might never be written, but her father so much enjoyed his hours of research that she took care not to voice her doubts; besides, it gave him something to do when the weather interfered with his gardening.

She left early in the morning, in the MG which had been a present from her godmother on her twenty-first birthday and her most treasured possession, for it was a means of getting home for a weekend at least once a month as well as for her holidays. She was a good driver and a fast one, so once over the winding road which crossed Woodbury Common she joined the main road and put her foot down. She was on duty the next morning, and she wanted an hour or two to settle in once more before she went on the ward. Her brain was already busy with the work ahead of her; there would be two new student nurses to absorb into the staff of the Men's Surgical ward she had been running for two years now; her staff nurse would need—and deserve—a long weekend off; there was that little tussle with Matron before her, concerning the new ward curtains—and there was Clive Barton, the Surgical Registrar, who had shown signs of becoming serious about her, and for some reason she couldn't quite understand, she didn't want to encourage him. Which was silly really, for she liked him very much, perhaps she was a little fond of him even and might get fonder, but she hesitated to commit herself.

She whizzed past a couple of slow-moving transports, wondering why it was that Lucy, quiet and retiring and shy, who had little or no opportunity of meeting any men, should have known the moment she had set eyes upon David that she wanted to marry him.

Charity's dark winged eyebrows drew together in a frown. Perhaps she was never going to meet a man who would make her feel like that—willing to hand over her whole life without question. She slowed down to go through Axminster, to get caught up in the early morning traffic filtering its way through the narrow, curling main street. She glanced at her watch; she was doing nicely, she would stop for lunch just before she got on to the M3 and then press on, for London would take a bit of getting through even outside the rush hour.

She reached St Simon's Hospital in time to join her friends in the Sisters' sitting-room for an early tea. They hailed her with pleasure and a spate of questions about her holiday, brought her up to date with the hospital news and settled down to drink their tea and eat as much bread and butter and jam as time allowed.

"Did anything exciting happen, Charity?" Nancy Benson wanted to know as she got up to fill her cup.

Charity sat down on the arm of the chair. "No—at least, not exciting, exactly; a man fainted while we were waiting to cross one of the ferries—an American, Mr Arthur C. Boekerchek..." There was a shriek of laughter. "Yes, I know it's a gorgeous name, isn't it—I couldn't believe my ears."

"I suppose you did your Florence Nightingale act?" a small girl remarked, "or was there a doctor around?"

Charity, a little belatedly, discovered that she didn't want to tell anyone about the doctor. She said briskly: "Oh, yes—someone or other came along, and the American was taken to a hotel to rest. It wasn't in the least exciting. Tell me, how is our Alice doing with Mr Wright?"

"Our Alice" was Accident Room Sister, a quiet retiring girl in her early thirties. Her younger colleagues had despaired of her seeming content to remain single, and when Mr Wright, the assistant radiologist, equally quiet and retiring, had shown interest in her, they had combined in a conspiracy to bring them together as often as possible. Her inquiry was met with a triumphant cry of: "They're engaged—isn't it marvellous? After all our hard work and patience."

"I wonder who'll be next?" asked Nancy, and looked at Charity, who said instantly and strongly: "Don't look at me—I've no one in mind," which wasn't quite true, but how could one be serious about a man one had glimpsed for the briefest moment of time and would never see again?

They dispersed very soon after that, most of them to go back on to their wards, the lucky ones off duty to change for an evening out, and Charity to her room to unpack and get ready for the morning.

She had only been away a fortnight, but there were a number of new patients, although old Mr Grey, who had been in the ward for some time, was still there, as were Mr Timms and Charlie Green. During her absence, she noticed, they had contrived to get moved into the four-bedded, partitioned area at the top of the ward where doubtless they were continuing their cosy little card parties whenever it was possible to get someone to push their beds together. There was a fourth man there, and she passed from her patients' glad cries of welcome to his bed—a small, cherubic-faced elderly man, recovering from a not too serious operation, and, as Charlie was quick to tell her, a tip-top rummy player. She smiled at them in a motherly fashion, begged them to be good boys and went on down the ward.

The patients here were all new, so she began the task of getting to know them—twenty-odd men who had been admitted during her fortnight's absence—supported after a while by her staff nurse, Lacey Bell, who presently, at Charity's invitation, followed her into her office, where they drank their coffee together while Lacey added a few details about the patients—details best left unsaid in the ward. She was a good nurse, thought Charity, listening to her astute sum-ming-up of the cases, and one day she would make a good Sister—perhaps she already had aspirations to step into her own shoes. Charity was very well aware that the hospital expected her to marry Clive Barton.

She gathered her scattered thoughts together and said cheerfully: "Thanks, Lacey, you've done a good job while I've been away." She smiled at the girl opposite her. "How about a weekend off? I'm sure you've some overtime to work off."

Her staff nurse looked pleased. "Lovely, thank you, Sister, if you're sure it's OK." She got up. "I'll just go and make sure the ward's straight, shall I?"

Charity nodded. "Do—I'll flip through these notes,

and mind you're at hand during Mr Howard's round, I may need a reminder.''

She had never needed a reminder yet, thought Lacey as she swung down the ward once more. Sister Dawson might be one of the most eye-catching girls at St Simon's, she was also one of the brainiest; she had never been known to forget anything; she learned new techniques within minutes and she had been the Gold Medalist of her year—a sufficiency of talents to swell her pretty head, and yet they hadn't; she never mentioned her medal, nor for that matter had she ever been heard to tell anyone that she had the Advanced Driver's Certificate, could speak fluent French and passable German, even if with a strong English accent; that she swam like a fish and played a first-class game of tennis, and had received more proposals of marriage than any other female in the hospital.

She deserved better than Clive Barton, mused her faithful staff nurse, plumping up pillows and straightening counterpanes while she kept a stern eye on the student nurses. Clive was all right, but Charity Dawson needed someone even cleverer than she was and with a brain just that much quicker; someone to be the boss, however gently he did it. Lacey, reviewing the eligible males to hand, couldn't discover one who might do. It vexed her so that she spoke rather more sharply than she had intended to Mr Grey, and then had to tell him she hadn't meant a word of it.

Charity, left alone, started on the notes, she read

them fast and carefully and when she was half way through them, got up to peer at herself in the small mirror behind her desk. She was by no means vain, but no ward Sister would wish to do a round with one of the consultant surgeons, with her pleated muslin cap at an incorrect angle; she adjusted her headgear minutely, wrinkled her nose at her reflection, and sat down again. She was studying the last of the notes when Clive Barton came in.

Charity raised her green eyes for a moment and smiled. "Hi," she said briefly, "I shan't be a tick—there's some cool coffee on the tray and a mug behind you."

She bent her head again while her companion did as she had suggested and then took the chair opposite her. He was a middle-sized young man, with a pleasant face and pale hair already receding a little. He looked to be a mild man too, but Charity knew that there was a good deal of determination behind his placid features. Clive wanted to get to the top—to become a consultant—he had been a registrar for several years now and was liked and respected by the consultants he worked for. Sooner or later one of them would retire, and he, if he was lucky, would have a chance of stepping into his shoes. He sat quietly now, admiring Charity; he was almost in love with her, he certainly liked her enormously and she would make him a splendid wife. Besides, she was known to all the consultants and a great many of the local GP's and they liked her, a fact which would be of considerable help to him. She was certainly a good-looker, although he had sometimes wished that she weren't so clever. Not that she ever paraded the fact; there was no need, it was so obvious, and he had never quite liked her hair, it was so vivid, and somehow the simple knot she wore above her slender neck made it all the more so. A vague longing to change her into someone smaller and meeker and less spectacular entered his head, to be instantly dismissed as treason; Charity was a darling girl; he made the thought positive by asking: "How about coming out this evening? I'm sick of canteen food."

She slapped the notes tidily together and smiled across the desk at him. "I'd love to—how I loathe coming back—it seems worse than usual."

"Meet anyone interesting?" he asked her idly, and because she sensed that he didn't really want to know, she was able to say composedly: "Father's friends." Her ear had caught the sound of feet. "Here's Mr Howard."

The round went off well; Mr Howard was in good spirits, which meant, naturally enough, that those who accompanied him were in good spirits too, even though they were forced to listen to his often-told jokes, but better that than the sharp questions he fired at them; medical students who so often regrettably gave the wrong answers.

There were no operations that day; the routine of

dressings, getting patients up who didn't want to get up, and keeping in bed those who were determined to get out of it, conducting Miss Evans, the Principal Nursing Officer, round the ward, dealing with various housemen, physiotherapists, visitors and those of her staff who wanted her private ear for some reason or other, kept Charity busy until she went off duty at five o'clock. She was to meet Clive at seven; there was plenty of time to bath and change, so she went along to the sitting-room and ate her tea in company with such of her friends who were off duty too, talking shop as usual, and presently went upstairs to her pleasant little room.

Clive hadn't told her where they were going, she supposed it would be the quiet little restaurant close to the hospital where they had been several times before. She chose the lime green wild silk with its matching jacket and brushed her chestnut hair until it shone, before running downstairs to meet him at the Home entrance. She hoped uneasily that he wasn't going to ask her to marry him; he had started to once before and she had gently dissuaded him, knowing that she was only postponing the inevitable.

She wasn't even sure what she was going to say when he did propose; she was attracted to him, perhaps she was a little in love with him, but she didn't think the feeling was enough to last a lifetime. Love, she felt sure, should sweep one off one's feet, and leave one uncaring about anything or anybody else, and Clive hadn't done that—besides, she wasn't even sure that he loved her. She had no conceit, but she couldn't help but be aware that she was a striking-looking girl, one whom men liked to be seen out with; she was also aware that she had intelligence as well as looks. She sighed and shrugged and then smiled at Clive waiting patiently in the hospital courtyard.

They dined pleasantly together, and over coffee he asked her to marry him, and looking at his earnest face across the table, she very nearly said yes. Only a fleeting memory, the tail-end of a dream, of a laconic giant of a man who didn't like her accent, prevented her. But because Clive was so persistent, she did promise to think it over.

"I have to be quite certain," she told him. "You see, when I marry it will be for the rest of my life—oh, I understand that sometimes divorce is inevitable, but perhaps it could sometimes be prevented if the people concerned had been quite sure before they married." She grinned engagingly. "Aren't I a pompous ass? I'm bossy too, you know—you might hate that."

She hoped that he would say something about making sure that she would never get the chance to boss him, but he didn't, only smiled and said that he wouldn't mind—a remark which strangely disquieted her.

It was when they were leaving the restaurant that a girl ahead of them fell in the foyer. Both Charity

and Clive went to help her, for the girl's companion
was elderly and stout and past bending. The girl was
a wisp of a thing, slim and golden-haired and blue-
eyed, who to Charity's faint disgust, gave way at once
to easy tears even as she assured Clive prettily that
she had only tripped and not hurt herself in the least.
And Charity, glancing at Clive's face, could see that
he rather liked this feminine display of helplessness,
a disquieting thought, for she had been brought up to
control her feelings in public and reserve her tears for
the privacy of her own room, something she had
sometimes found difficult when she had longed to
have a good cry without having to wait until she was
by herself, when quite often, by that time, she had no
wish to weep any more. But this pretty little creature
she was supporting now had no such inhibitions; she
cried with ease and charm so that Charity felt com-
pelled to suggest that they should retire to the powder
room and repair the damage, if there was any.

The girl cheered up under Charity's kindly eye, introduced herself as Margery Cross, and after a few
minutes of re-doing her face, followed Charity back
into the foyer where the two gentlemen were chatting
quite happily together. There was another round of
introductions before Margery thanked Clive with all
the fervour of one who had been rescued from untold
horrors, and with several backward glances, accompanied the stout gentleman, who it turned out was her
doting father, to the taxi waiting for them. Charity

stood patiently beside Clive while he waited on the pavement, staring after it until it had disappeared round a corner, before taking her arm and starting on their walk back to the hospital.

"Poor child," he remarked. "It's so unusual to find someone so sensitive in these days; most girls are so self-sufficient."

"They have to be," said Charity mildly.

He glanced at her quickly. "You were a dear, taking her under your wing like that—her father was most grateful. That's what I like about you, Charity, you always know what to do."

But she didn't, she told him silently; she didn't know if she wanted to marry him, did she? And if she had known what to do at Vlissingen, she would have found a way of talking—even for a few minutes—to that doctor who remained so persistently in her thoughts, just to convince him that she wasn't a priggish English girl, boastful about her knowledge of German and resentful of his criticism. She admitted now that it was his complete unawareness of her which had so annoyed her, and if she were to be quite honest, she might as well admit at the same time that she didn't dislike him. On the contrary.

"You're very silent," observed Clive. "I expect you're tired, Charity."

She agreed with him; not tired in the least, but it would be easier to agree than try to explain that she felt, all of a sudden, dissatisfied with life. They parted at the entrance to the Home and Clive kissed her goodnight, and although she enjoyed it, as any normal girl would, she felt no stirring within her. The fact frightened her a little as she got ready for bed. Perhaps she would never love anyone; some people had no great depth of feeling, supposing she should be one of these unfortunates? She went to sleep finally, worrying about it.

She had been back for two weeks when Miss Evans sent for her soon after eight o'clock on a day which bade fair to be both hot and busy. Theatre day, and the temperature already in the seventies. Charity muttered under her breath, bade the invaluable Lacey Bell take over, and sped through the hospital to its very heart where the PNO had her office, ringed about by lesser nursing officers whose duty it was to hold back those too eager to take up her time. But today Charity received no rebuff, no delay even, she was swept through to Miss Evans' sanctum before she had time to do more than straighten her cap and adjust her cuffs. She had no idea why she had been sent for and there had been no moment in which to review the happenings of the last few days to discover what she had done wrong. She braced herself, took up her position before the desk and wished her superior a good morning.

It was a surprise when Miss Evans smiled at her, a rather vinegary smile, it was true, but still a smile.

It was still more of a surprise when she was bidden to take a chair.

"I realise that you are busy," began Miss Evans, a shade pompously, "but there is a matter of importance concerning yourself which I must discuss with you without delay—an urgent matter, I might say, and somewhat unusual. I have received a visit from a member of the American Embassy staff this morning with the request that you should be released from your duties here in order to nurse a member of their trade delegation in The Hague." Her rather cold eyes studied Charity's quiet face with interest. "A Mr Arthur C. Boekerchek—an extraordinary name—I understand that you have already met him."

Charity felt surprise and excitement and kept both feelings firmly under control. "He fainted in a car at the ferry—I did very little, I just happened to be there…"

Miss Evans held up a hand. "The details are irrelevant, Sister. I merely wished to know that you were indeed the person they ask for, although it is a puzzle to me that it must be you and no one else—one would have thought that there was a sufficiency of nurses in a large city such as The Hague. However, I found it impossible to refuse their request on Mr Boekerchek's behalf without giving offence; you will be good enough to make ready to leave for Holland some time tomorrow."

Charity's green eyes glinted dangerously. "But

perhaps I might not wish to go to Holland, Miss Evans,'' she prompted gently. ''I wasn't aware that I had been asked.''

Her superior's face went a rich puce; at any moment, thought Charity naughtily, she'll begin to gobble—she had never liked Miss Evans; few of her staff did, she wasn't too good at her job, but she was nearing retirement; for the most part they allowed themselves to be dictated to and quietly went their own way without minding overmuch. But this time, Charity did mind. She got to her feet.

''I'm afraid that I must refuse to go, Miss Evans,'' she said politely. ''And now, if you will excuse me, I should go back to the ward—it's theatre day.''

She was immediately immersed in the tasks which awaited her—drips to supervise patients to send on time to the theatre, dressings to do, nurses to keep an eye on—she urged on her team of helpers, the faithful Bell at her right hand. There was certainly no time to think about her interview with Miss Evans; that she would hear more of it was a foregone conclusion. Which she did, very shortly and hardly in the manner which she would have expected.

The last case came down to the ward just after twelve o'clock. Mr Howard, whose operating day it was, worked fast and expected everyone else to do the same; he arrived hard on the heels of his patient, still in his theatre trousers and a terrible old sweater, his cap pulled untidily over his hair, his mask dragged down under his chin. He marched up the ward to where Charity was connecting the quiet form in bed to the various tubes vital to his recovery, and said impatiently: "Morning, girl—I'll see that first case—wasn't very happy about him."

They were bending over the unconscious man when Mr Howard asked: "What's all this I hear about you going to Holland, eh?"

Charity reconnected a tube and said with calm: "Matron had arranged for me to go, but I refused."

He let out a barking laugh. "Did you now? Why?"

"I was told nothing about it until the arrangements had been made. That annoyed me, sir."

They had moved on to the second of the patients and Mr Howard was deep in his notes when a student nurse slid silently to Charity's side.

"There's someone to see you, Sister," she breathed, "he says it's important. He's an American."

Mr Howard, for all his sixty years, had splendid hearing. "Run along, girl," he advised Charity. "I don't doubt you're about to get a handsome apology, so you can come down off your high horse and offer your services, after all." He cast her a quick, friendly look. "Not that I shan't miss you."

"How did you know...?" began Charity, and was told to hush and get on with it and leave the student nurse, pale with fright, in her place.

The man waiting for her was elderly, with a narrow, clever face and a penetrating voice which he strove to quieten out of deference to the patients. He wasted no time after he had introduced himself. "If I might have a word?" he begged, and on being shown into Charity's office and bidden to sit, did so.

"I've come to apologise, my dear young lady," he began. "I had no idea that you had been told nothing of our request—indeed, I was led to suppose that you knew of it and had consented to go." He coughed gently. "However, the—er—misunderstanding has been put right, and I hope that if I ask you personally to come as nurse to our Mr Boekerchek, you will agree to do so."

He was rather nice, despite his American accent and enormous horn-rimmed spectacles—he reminded her of Mr Boekerchek, they both had nice smiles. She found herself smiling in return. "I'll come whenever you want me to," she told him, and was surprised at herself for saying it. "Miss Evans told me that you had asked if I would leave tomorrow."

He nodded. "It is an urgent matter, if you could arrange to go to The Hague as soon as possible. Mr Boekerchek has a rare condition—multiple insuli-nomata—the fainting fit which he experienced when you so kindly went to his aid was an early symptom of it, I believe. When he was told yesterday that surgery was imperative, he agreed to undergo it on con-dition that you could be found to act as his nurse."

He grinned engagingly. "He is certain that you will bring him good luck."

Charity was thinking about multiple insulinomata, and trying to remember all she knew about it. She had only seen two or three cases of it and none of them had recovered—she recollected the squint and the tingling hands and knew now why they had aroused her interest; they were two of the earliest symptoms. Probably Mr Boekerchek's condition had been discovered in good time; she enjoyed a challenge, if she could, and she would do everything to help him to make a complete recovery. "I'll do my best," she told her visitor. "I can be ready by tomorrow and if possible I should like to drive myself, only I've no papers for the car."

He brushed that aside. "That can easily be attended to. If you will let me know what time you intend to leave, everything will be arranged and all you need will be sent here to you this evening."

She blinked. "How nice—there's a ferry leaving at midday from Dover." She added doubtfully, "It's the holiday season…"

"Don't worry about that." He was comfortably efficient; obviously she was to have no worries on the journey. He left in another five minutes, the tiresome details dealt with, leaving her with nothing further to do but pack; fill up with petrol and telephone home, all of which she was forced to do that evening when she came off duty, having had not a moment to call her own until then.

She didn't see Miss Evans again before she left, a message telling her to take what uniform she needed with her, and to notify the Office as soon as she knew the date of her return, was all the official acknowledgment she received of her departure, an omission easily made up for by the enthusiastic help of her friends, who assisted her to pack, provided the odds and ends she had had no time to purchase for herself, and even volunteered to tell Clive, whom she had completely forgotten in the excitement of the moment. She dashed off a note to him the next morning just before she left and then forgot about him almost immediately.

CHAPTER TWO

IT WAS A smooth journey, even if crowded, but Charity hardly noticed that; she was immersed in a copy of *The Lancet* she had borrowed from Mr Howard after she had asked him urgently on the previous afternoon to tell her all he could about her patient's complaint.

"Oh, so you're going after all?" he had snorted at her. "I can do better than tell you, there was a first-class article about it in last week's *Lancet*." And he had brought it down to the ward that evening, when he came to do a final check of his patients.

She studied it now, learning it almost word for word, so that later on she would know what everyone was talking about. It was a well-written article, written by a professor at the Utrecht School of Medicine, a certain Everard van Tijlen, a man, she considered, reading it through for the last time, who knew what he was about—a fine decisive style and sound knowledge of the subject. She put it away in her case and went up on deck to watch the flat coast of Belgium creep nearer.

She made good time from Zeebrugge to the Hague; it was only a little after seven o'clock when she drew up smartly before the address she had been given. The block of flats was large and modern and obviously luxurious and in a pleasant part of the city. She wasted no time, but got out, locked the car, went into the foyer and asked to be taken to the fifth floor by the porter.

Mr Arthur C. Boekerchek lived in style, she discovered when his apartment door was opened by a small woman with an unhappy face; the hall was large and square and furnished with taste and there seemed to be passages and doors leading off in all directions. The woman smiled uncertainly.

"Oh, are you the English nurse?"

Charity smiled and said that yes, she was. This, unless she was very much mistaken, was Mr Boekerchek's wife. "I'm sorry to arrive so late," she apologised. "If I could just put my car away and get my luggage…"

Her hostess went back to the door where the porter still lingered and spoke to him and then turned to Charity. "If you would let him have the keys," she suggested, "he'll put the car away—there's an underground garage—and bring up your cases," and when Charity had done this and closed the door the poor lady burst into tears.

"I never thought you'd come," she sobbed, "and Arthur was so dead set on having you and no one else, and I thought if you wouldn't come, he'd refuse surgery and then what would happen?"

Charity put an arm round the little lady's shoulders and led her across the hall to a half-opened door which she hoped was a sitting-room. She was right, it was. She settled Mrs Boekerchek in a chair and sat down close by. "But I am here," she pointed out cheerfully, "and we'll have your husband on his feet again in no time at all."

Her companion sniffed, blew her nose and made a great effort to calm down. "I don't know what I expected," she confided, "but you're quite different, I reckon—no wonder Arthur wouldn't budge." She got up quickly. "There, see what an old fool I am—you must be tired to death and I'm wasting your time. There's a meal for you—I'll get Nel to serve it..."

Charity had got to her feet too. "That sounds lovely, but could I have five minutes to tidy myself and then go and see Mr Boekerchek? Will his doctor be coming this evening?"

"No—tomorrow morning. He's to go to Utrecht, you know. The ambulance is coming at nine o'clock to take him to the hospital there—I've forgotten its name—Dr Donker said he'd see you before you went." She was leading the way across the hall again and into one of the passages. "This is your room. I hope you'll be comfortable—there's a shower room beyond. Shall I come back for you in a few minutes?" She sounded wistful; Charity guessed that she needed company to take her mind off her husband's illness.

"Give me ten minutes," she agreed readily.

The room was luxurious; a pity, thought Charity, tidying herself hastily, that she would only have one night here. After that it would presumably be the Nurses' Home in Utrecht. She fancied that it might be very like the Home at St Simon's. She cast a lingering look round the room and turned to smile at Mrs Boekerchek at the door.

Mr Boekerchek certainly looked ill. He was pale and decidedly irritable despite his pleasure at seeing Charity. He had lost a lot of weight too, and confided to her that he was quite unable to work any more and suffered from a depression which was a blight both to himself and his wife.

"Hyperinsulinism, that's my trouble," he declared, "that professor what's-his-name who's going to carve me up, explained it to me—can't say I made head or tail of it, though. But I trust him all right—lucky I'd already met him." He managed a thin smile. "Just as long as you know what he's talking about, eh? I'm glad they got hold of you. I do declare that I wouldn't have agreed to surgery unless they had. I'm a daft old man, aren't I? but thank God, I'm important enough to be humoured."

Charity stayed with him for the rest of the evening, studying the notes the doctor had left for her before settling him for the night, eating a hasty supper and then going to sit for half an hour with his wife, whom she tried, not very successfully, to comfort before going to her room and bed. It seemed to her that her head had barely touched the pillow before Nel was shaking her awake with a cup of tea on a tray and the news that it was six o'clock, something the city's carillons let her know, a dozen times over.

Mindful of the doctor's visit at eight o'clock, she dressed, in uniform this time—and went along to her patient's room. He had slept well, he told her, and was positively cheerful at the idea of getting things going at last. She helped him wash and shave, made sure that he was comfortable, checked his packed case, and went along to the kitchen. Mrs Boekerchek was up too, fussing round the stolid Nel while she prepared their breakfast. Mr Boekerchek, naturally enough, had very little appetite. Charity saw to his wants first and then made a healthily sustaining meal herself while her companion drank quantities of scalding coffee and jumped up and down like a yo-yo. She wasn't going to Utrecht with them; Charity was to telephone her later on in the day, and tell her what had been decided, and when the decision to operate had been taken she would go over to the hospital and stay if it were considered necessary.

Charity discussed Mrs Boekerchek's plans at length and in a cheerful voice and was rewarded by seeing the unhappy little woman's face brighten. "Wear something pretty when you come," she advised her, "something your husband likes; it will help him enormously, you know, if he's feeling weak and ill, to see you looking pretty and nicely dressed—and don't be upset when you see him after the op. He'll look very pale and strange and there'll be tubes and things all over the place—they look dramatic, but he won't notice them, so don't you either.''

Her words had the desired effect. Mrs Boekerchek fell to planning various outfits and even pondered the advisability of a visit to the hairdresser. ''I have a rinse, you know,'' she confided. ''It needs to be done every week or so—Arthur is dead set on me not going grey, I reckon.'' She eyed Charity's burnished head with some envy. ''Yours is real, I guess,'' she asked wistfully.

''Well, yes,'' Charity felt almost apologetic about it, ''but quite often people think it isn't.'' Her pretty mouth curved in a smile. ''Do you mind if I go to my room and make sure everything is ready? We mustn't keep the ambulance waiting and I'm not certain how long the doctor will take—it's almost eight o'clock.''

He came a few minutes later, a small dark man with thick glasses and hair brushed carefully over the bald spot on the top of his head. He spoke English with a fluency she instantly envied and plunged at once into instructions, details of his patient's illness, and dire warnings as to what might go wrong and what she was to do if they did. She listened attentively, collected the necessary papers he had entrusted to her care, wished him goodbye and rejoined her patient.

Ten minutes later they were in the ambulance, on their way to Utrecht.

It was a journey of forty miles or so, and since they travelled on the motorway for almost the entire distance and the ambulance was an elegant sleek model built for speed, they were soon on the outskirts of the city, but here their progress slowed considerably, and Charity, bent on keeping her patient's mind on the normal things of life, encouraged him to describe the city to her, and looked when told to do so through the dark glass windows, trying to identify the various buildings he was telling her about. He had become quite cheerful during their ride together and had told her about his work and his family and home in the USA.

"This country's OK," he told her, "but a bit cramped, I guess—why, you can drive from one end to the other in the matter of a few hours, now, back home..." He paused. "I guess it's OK, though, like I said—nice people no need to learn the language, and a good thing too, for it's a tongue-twister, all right. Where are we now?"

Charity had a look. "Going up a narrow lane, walls on either side—the backs of houses I should think. Oh, here's a gate and a courtyard—I believe it's the hospital."

She was right. The ambulance passed the main entrance and drew up before a double swing door. Within minutes Mr Boekerchek was stretched tidily under his blankets on a trolley and they were making their way through the corridors and vast areas filled with crowded benches—Outpatients Charity guessed, and wished that there was more time to look around her. They were in a lift by now, though, on their way up to the sixth floor.

The lift door swung open on to a square hall which opened in its turn into a wide corridor. Someone must have given warning of their arrival, for there was a youngish woman in uniform waiting for them.

She smiled as she shook hands. "Hoofd Zuster Doelsma," she volunteered. "Charity Dawson," said Charity, not sure what to call herself, "and this is Mr Arthur C. Boekerchek."

They proceeded smoothly down the corridor, lined with doors along one side and with great glass windows, giving one an excellent view of the wards beyond them, on the other. Half-way down Zuster Doelsma opened a door, revealing a small bright room with a modicum of furniture and a very up-to-date bed. Piped oxygen, intercom, sucker, intensive care equipment—Charity's sharp eyes registered their presence with satisfaction; there was everything she might need. There was a small, comfortable chair close to the bed and a compact desk and stool facing it, and cupboards built into one wall; she would examine them presently. Now she turned her attention to settling her patient comfortably in his bed, much cheered by the appearance of a little nurse bearing a tray with two cups of coffee on it. Sipping it together, she and her companion decided that the room was nice, that Zuster Doelsma looked friendly, that the hospital, in fact, was very much like the most modern of American hospitals which Mr Boekerchek could call to mind.

He was in the middle of telling her so when the door opened and the giant from Vlissingen walked in, closely attended by his registrar, a houseman and Zuster Doelsma. Charity stood and stared at him with her mouth open, watching as he went to the bed, shook Mr Boekerchek by the hand, spoke briefly and then turned round to face her. If she had been surprised to see him, he most certainly was not. He gave her a cool nod, offered a firm hand and remarked: "Ah, the English Miss Dawson, come to stay with us for a little while. An opportunity for you to demonstrate your talent for languages; you should acquire a smattering of Dutch during that period."

She felt her cheeks warm under his quizzical look and checked a childish urge to shout something rude at him. Instead she said in what she hoped was a cool voice: "I think there will be no need of that, Professor, for my Dutch would probably turn out to be as bad as your manners."

They were standing a little apart from the others; she watched his eyes narrow as a smile touched the corner of his straight mouth. "So we are to cross swords, Miss Dawson?" he wanted to know softly.

"Well, it seems likely," she told him sturdily, "though not during working hours, naturally."

His laugh of genuine amusement took her by surprise. "A pity," he observed, "for we shall have little opportunity of meeting."

She didn't answer him, for she was fighting disappointment; she had wanted to meet this man again, even though she had never admitted it even to herself, and now, by some quirk of fate, here he was, and obviously not sharing her feelings, indeed, very much the reverse. She promised herself then and there that she would make him change his opinion of her; and this satisfying thought was interrupted by his:

"You look very pleased with yourself about something. Now, supposing we have a talk with the patient."

She could see within minutes that here was a man who knew his job. He had a measured way of speaking, although he was never at a loss for a word and he was completely confident in himself and the results of the operation he intended to perform, without being boastful. It was also equally apparent to her that whatever his private feelings were towards herself, he had no intention of allowing them to influence their relationship as surgeon and nurse, for when he had talked to Mr Boekerchek he drew her on one side and his manner when he spoke was pleasantly friendly with no hint of mockery or dislike. "I shall want you in theatre," he told her. "I shall operate at one o'clock tomorrow afternoon and you will be good enough to adjust your duty hours so that you will be available until midnight of that day. You are conversant with intensive care?''

''Yes, Professor.''

He nodded. ''You will be directly responsible to me for all the nursing care of Mr—er—Boekerchek. I know that you will be unable to be here all the time, and a nurse has been seconded to share your duties. But please understand that I shall hold you responsible. I will explain…''

Which he did, and at some length, and she listened carefully, storing away facts and techniques and his way of doing things, because he would expect her to know them all.

''You have nursed these cases before?''

''Two—not recently, though. I read your article in *The Lancet*.''

There was a brief gleam of amusement in his eyes. ''Indeed? I had no idea that *The Lancet* was read by anyone other than my own profession.''

He was needling her again, but she kept her cool, saying quietly:

''The consultant surgeon for whom I work at St Simon's lent it to me. I had no idea that it was you…''

''Why should you?'' he asked coolly, and turned to go. ''You will be in theatre at five to one tomorrow, Sister Dawson.''

She was kept busy for the rest of the day; Mr Boekerchek was to undergo a series of tests, which meant a constant flow of path lab people in and out, And he had to be X-rayed too, an expedition upon which she accompanied him, as well as being seen by various other people connected with his future well-being; the anaesthetist, a youngish man, darkly good-looking and with a charm of manner which Charity was sure must endear him to his patients. He was charming to her too, speaking English, of course, like almost everyone else in the hospital. The professor's nasty remark had been quite unnecessary and it still rankled; she registered a resolve not to learn or speak a word of Dutch, happily forgetful that she would be the one to suffer from her resolution, not he, and turned to smile at another caller, the professor's registrar, a short, rather stout young man with a round, cheerful face and a habit of quoting his chief on every possible occasion.

"You will find the operation most interesting," he assured Charity, standing in the corridor outside her patient's room. "Professor van Tijlen is outstanding in surgery, you know, and this particular operation is of his own technique—he has done already one dozen and they live yet."

Charity said tartly: "Marvellous—what else does he specialise in?"

"All illnesses of the stomach and the—the gut."

"Big deal," she observed flippantly, and at the

look of uncertainty upon her companion's face hastened to explain: "That's just an expression in English. It means how—how marvellous."

Mr van Dungen looked mollified. "He is a wonderful man," he told her sternly, and then smiled. "You will perhaps call me Dof?"

"Of course. My name's Charity." They smiled at each other like old friends and she added: "I say, you'll help me out if I get in a jam, won't you?" and had to repeat it all again differently, explaining that getting into a jam didn't mean quite what it sounded like.

Mrs Boekerchek came over that evening, rather grandly in an Embassy car with a chauffeur who followed her to the door of the patient's room with a great quantity of flowers and several baskets of fruit which Mr Boekerchek would be unable to eat. Charity soothed his anxious wife and went to fetch Dof van Dungen, whose cheerful manner and sometimes uncertain English might put her patient's better half at her ease far more than technical details of the operation. It gave her a brief breathing space too, to find Zuster Doelsma; she hadn't been to the Nurses' Home yet, a large, gloomy-looking building at the far end of the hospital courtyard. It was a good chance to slip over now, the Dutch girl agreed; she would lend a nurse for a few minutes to show her the way to her room.

"Tomorrow we treat you better, Sister Dawson,"

she said kindly. "Today is bad, no time to yourself, for I must ask you to stay on duty until the night nurse comes on, but tomorrow do not come on duty until ten o'clock, so that you will have an hour or two to yourself. I think that Professor van Tijlen told you that he wishes that you stay on duty until midnight; it is better for the patient, you understand? It will be a long day for you, but there is a good nurse to relieve you, and after the first day it will be easier. Now if you wish to go to your room? and when you return we will go to supper together."

Fair enough, thought Charity, accompanying the little nurse detailed to take her to the Home where she was delighted to find its dull exterior concealed a very modern and bright interior. Her room was on the fourth floor in the Sisters' wing, an airy, fair-sized room, nicely furnished and with the luxury of a shower concealed in one of its cupboards. The little nurse, whose English was fragmental, having pointed out this amenity with some pride, grinned, said *"Dag, Zuster,"* and scuttled off, leaving Charity to tidy herself. She would have liked time to unpack, but it seemed she was to have none for the moment; she wasted no time therefore in getting back to the ward, where she found Zuster Doelsma bowed over the Kardex.

"I'll just go and see Mr Boekerchek," Charity suggested. "When do you want me back?"

"Supper in ten minutes," the Dutch girl smiled at her. "That is a funny name which your patient has."

Charity chuckled. "Yes, I expect his ancestors came from Russia, but the Arthur C. makes it very American, though, doesn't it?"

Mrs Boekerchek was on the point of leaving. "But I'll be here tomorrow—about six o'clock, that nice young doctor said." She looked anxiously at Charity. "You'll be here, won't you, honey?"

Charity assured her that she would. "I'm coming on a little later in the morning and I shall stay with Mr Boekerchek until quite late in the evening, and there's a very good nurse to relieve me at night, so don't worry, everything will be fine."

Her companion's pleasant elderly face crumpled and then straightened itself at the warning: "Now, baby," from the bed, and Charity turned her back and busied herself with the flowers, thinking that she wouldn't much like to be addressed as baby, not by anyone—anyone at all; the professor was hardly a man to address anyone endearingly... She checked her galloping thoughts, telling herself that she must be tired indeed to allow such nonsense to creep into her head, and bestirred herself to accompany Mrs Boekerchek to the lift at the end of the corridor, where the little lady clasped both her hands and asked: "It is going to be OK, isn't it, honey?"

"Of course," Charity sounded very certain of it.

"Professor van Tijlen is just about the best surgeon for this particular operation, you know."

Her companion nodded. "I'm sure he is—such a dear kind man, too. He came today and explained to me just why he had to operate on Arthur, and when I cried like the old silly I am, he was so comforting. I trust him completely."

Charity, diverted by her speculations concerning the professor comforting anyone; made haste to answer and was a little surprised to hear herself agreeing wholeheartedly with Mrs Boekerchek, and still more surprised to find that she believed what she was saying, too.

She met a number of the Dutch Sisters at supper; they all spoke English in varying degrees of fluency and she found herself with more invitations to do this, that and the other than she could ever hope to have time for, so that she went back to Mr Boekerchek quite cheered up; even if she wouldn't have much time to go out, at least the other girls were friendly.

She set about the routine of getting her patient ready for the night and when the night nurse, one Willa Groene, arrived, a sturdy fair-haired girl of about her own age, she relinquished him to her with a relief which, though concealed, was none the less real. It had been a long day—and a surprising one, she reminded herself as she was on the verge of sleep.

Mr Boekerchek wasn't in a good humour when she reached his room the next morning. His surly

"What's good about it?" in answer to her own greeting told her all she needed to know. His surliness, she had no doubt, hid a nasty attack of nerves; that terrible last-minute rebellion against a fate which had decreed that the only way out was to trust the surgeon. She had encountered it a hundred times: it passed swiftly but she had learned to help it on its way. She began the task of doing just that. There was quite a lot to do before they went to theatre; and she began, with cheerful calm, to do the numerous little jobs which would lead finally to his premed, talking unhurriedly for most of the time, pretending not to notice his silence, and after a while her patience was rewarded; he asked about her room in the Nurses' Home and was she being well treated?

"Like a queen," she assured him, and led the conversation cunningly away from hospital. She had succeeded in making him laugh, telling him about the professor's Lamborghini and her father's opinion of those who travelled in such splendid cars, when she realized that there was a third person in the room—the professor, filling the doorway with his bulk and looking as though he had been there for some time. He had.

"Your father's stricture makes me feel every year of my age," he remarked good-humouredly as he advanced to the bedside. "My only excuse for driving a Lamborghini is that I was given one when I was twenty-one, and twenty years later I haven't found a car I like better."

"What about a Chrysler?" asked his patient, quite diverted from his own troubles.

"A good car—but I think that I am now getting too old to change." He stared at the wall, thinking his own thoughts. "Perhaps—if I were to marry—the Lamborghini is hardly a family car." His manner changed and he began at once to talk to Mr Boeker-chek, to such good effect that that gentleman remained cheerful until the moment he closed his eyes in the peaceful half-sleep induced by the injection Charity had given him.

The theatre, when they reached it, reminded her forcibly of quite another sort of theatre; there was the audience, peering down through the glass above their heads, and the instruments, while not the musical variety, tinkled musically as they were laid out in their proper places. Charity, who had remained with her patient in the anaesthetic room, his hand comfortably fast in hers, took up her position by the anaesthetist and watched Mr Boekerchek's unconscious form being arranged with due care upon the operating table. This done to Theatre Sister's satisfaction, a kind of hush fell upon the group of people arranged in a kind of tableau in the centre of the theatre.

Into this hush came Professor van Tijlen, dwarfing everyone present, his mask pulled up over his splendid nose so that only his eyes were visible. He paused

by the table, greeted Theatre Sister, said a few words
to his registrar, murmured briefly to his houseman,
hovering nervously, stared hard at Charity—a stare
which she returned in full measure—and turned his
attention to his patient.

Charity watched him make a neat paramedian in-
cision and then, stage by stage, demonstrate his actions to his audience. It was a pity that she couldn't
understand a word he said, but she was kept so busy
that it didn't really matter; blood sugar samples had
to be taken every fifteen minutes, blood pressures had
to be read, and the anaesthetist kept her on her toes
with his requirements. But she managed, all the same,
to see something of what was going on. The professor
was a good surgeon, with no pernickety ways; he was
relaxed too, even though his concentration was ab-
solute. There was a little sigh of satisfaction as he
found and removed the adenoma which had been the
cause of Mr Boekerchek's illness; he spent some time
searching for any more which might be there, with no
success—presumably everything was as it should be;
he began on his careful needlework and presently,
when that was finished, stood back to allow the other
two men to finish off the suturing. He left the theatre
as the anaesthetist slid a fine tube down Mr Boekerchek's nostril while Theatre Sister attended to the
dressing, and Charity, kept busy with odd jobs, didn't
see him go. For so large a man he moved in a very
self-effacing manner.

He turned up again, just as silently, half an hour later, when having got her patient into bed under his space blanket, checked the infusions of blood, dextrose saline and another, special solution, all located in various limbs and all running at a different rate; made sure that the cannula for the taking of blood samples was correctly fixed, and made certain that the blood pressure was being properly monitored, Charity was taking Mr Boekerchek's pulse.

Beyond giving her a laconic hullo, the professor had nothing to say to her, but bent at once over his patient. It was only when he had satisfied himself that everything was just as it should be that he straightened his long back and came to take the charts from the desk. "You are familiar with the nursing care?" He looked at her, smiling a little. "Am I insulting you? I don't mean to, but if there is anything you are not quite certain about I shall be glad to help you."

Very handsomely put, she had to admit. "Thank you—I'm fine at the moment, but I'll not hesitate to let you or Mr Van Dungen know if I'm worried."

He nodded. "One of us will be available for the next twenty-four hours. Start aspirating in an hour and a half, if you please, and give water as ordered as soon as the patient is conscious. You will have help as and when you require it, but I must emphasise that you are in charge of the case and are responsible to me and no one else. You understand?"

There was a lot to do during the next few hours,

but by the end of that time Charity had the satisfaction of seeing her patient sitting up against his pillows, the blanket discarded, nicely doped and doing exactly as he ought. She had been warned to send a message to the professor when Mrs Boekerchek arrived that evening; he arrived as she entered the room, her face held rigid in a smile which threatened to crack at any moment.

The professor glanced at Charity. "Go and get a cup of coffee," he told her. "I shall be here for ten minutes or so—stay in the duty room."

She went thankfully; she had been relieved for fifteen minutes for a hasty meal on a tray in the office, but now she longed for a cup of tea, but coffee it was and better than nothing.

She sat in the austere little room, her shoes kicked off, her cap pushed to the back of her head. There were still several hours to go before she could go off duty, but that didn't matter; Mr Boekerchek was out of his particular wood provided nothing happened to hinder him. She swallowed a second cup of coffee, straightened her cap, shoved her feet back into their shoes and went back along the corridor.

The professor was ready to leave, taking Mrs Boekerchek with him. She had been crying, for her husband was in no state to warn her not to. The tears started again as she saw Charity, whom she kissed soundly. "I'll never be able to thank you—you two beautiful people," she said with a gratitude which wrung Charity's kind heart, and was borne away by the professor, who, without a word to Charity, closed the door quietly as they went.

He opened it a minute later to say: "I should be obliged if you would come on duty at eight o'clock tomorrow morning. You will be relieved later in the day, but I prefer you to be here while Mr Boekerchek is ill. Naturally any time you have owing to you will be made up." He turned to go again. "Thank you for your assistance today, Sister Dawson." His goodnight was an afterthought as he closed the door once more.

He certainly had no intention of sparing her, but she fancied that he didn't spare himself either where his patients, important or otherwise, were concerned. She dismissed him from her mind and started on her duties once again until she was relieved by the night nurse at midnight. It had been a busy day; as she got wearily into bed she wondered if the professor was still up, making his silent way through the hospital, or whether he too was in bed. She tried to imagine where he lived—probably in one of the old houses they had passed coming to the hospital on the previous day. She began to think about him, yawned, then yawned again, and fell asleep.

CHAPTER THREE

THERE WAS no time to spare for any thought other than that required of her work the next day, Mr Boekerchek was doing nicely, but there was a multitude of tasks to be done and none of them could be skipped, skimped or done carelessly. She took blood sugars, aspirated, checked drips, kept her patient comfortable and under sedation. The professor came in the morning half an hour after she had taken over from the night nurse, and in the afternoon he came again, expressed his satisfaction, consulted with Mr van Dungen, and went away again. And at the end of a long day Mrs Boekerchek came with such an overflowing gratitude for what she called Charity's devotion to duty, that Charity was quite reconciled to the few brief moments which she had had to herself.

But the next day was better; Mr Boekerchek, in a positive tangle of tubes, drip flasks and drain bottles, was sitting out of bed, looking rather shrunken and pinched and surrounded by a veritable bower of flowers and with a background of get-well cards which Charity had pinned to the wall so that he could have something to look at while he lay in bed. The professor and Dof van Dungen had examined them too, wasting what she considered to be a great deal of time over it, instead of getting on with their examination of their patient. And on the day after that, free of almost all his tubes by now and feeling much more himself, Mr Boekerchek, sitting in his chair watching Charity making his bed, observed: "Why, honey, you've been here the whole day long and half the night, and heaven knows how long before that. You're here early in the morning and you're still here when I go to sleep. I do declare," he went on in a voice that wasn't quite as strong as it could have been, "I'll ask Professor van Tijlen if you can't have time off..."

"Indeed she can," said the professor, and because he had startled her, Charity gave him a cross look; he had a habit of coming and going with that silent speed which could be disconcerting—he ignored the look and went on smoothly: "You are much better, Mr Boekerchek; you may have a second visitor this evening—I suggest that Sister Dawson gets you back to bed at four o'clock when your wife comes so that you may receive your extra company in your bed. Zuster Doelsma will keep an eye on you for a few hours."

He turned to look at Charity. "Zuster Theatre asked me this morning if you would be free later on—she and some of the other Sisters are going to the cinema and want you to go with them. You would like that?"

She would like it very much. "Zuster Doelsma

won't mind?'' she queried. ''I don't think she reckoned on my going off duty for the first few days.''

He smiled faintly. ''She has reminded me already
that you are being treated most unfairly,'' he spoke
with impersonal kindness. ''Mr Boekerchek is sufficiently recovered for your hours of off duty to return
to normal, but these matters are best left to the ward
Sister, I find.''

Charity murmured a meek ''Yes, sir,'' feeling anything but meek; he somehow had conveyed the impression that she was a necessity to be put up with
for the time being—an alien in his smooth-running
hospital world. Her bosom heaved with her strong
feelings and she looked up to see him watching her
with a gleam in his eyes and a little smile touching
the corners of his mouth which made it obvious that
he had a shrewd idea of what she was thinking. She
said woodenly: ''You would like to see the charts,
Professor,'' and handed him the lot without waiting
for him to say he did.

It was delightful to change out of uniform and join
the small party of girls waiting for her in the pleasant
sitting-room on the ground floor. They absorbed her
into their circle with no effort at all; within half an
hour they were all walking through the busy streets,
taking it in turns to point out anything of interest to
her, until they reached the cinema. The film was a
German one, dubbed in Dutch. The girls on either
side of her carefully translated it for her; she didn't

mention that she could understand it very well for herself; there was a vague idea at the back of her mind that the professor might get to hear about it and mention it—nastily—next time they met.

They were out of the cinema by half past eight and were standing on the pavement, arguing as to the best café to which they could take Charity, when Tina, the theatre Sister, interrupted herself to say:

"Oh, look, there is Professor van Tijlen," and everyone stared into the street, where, halted by traffic lights, was a Daimler Sovereign with him at the wheel and a pretty, lint-haired girl beside him. Everyone—except Charity—waved, and he lifted a hand in a friendly wave as the car drew smoothly away.

"A new girl?" one of the girls wanted to know. "I have not seen her before. She is nice to look at, do you not think, Charity?"

"Extremely pretty." She didn't believe in half measures.

"He has a splendid taste," observed Tina admiringly. "It is such a pity that he does not fancy any of us—we have all done our best."

There was a little gust of laughter as they started off in the direction of the Esplanade Restaurant, which, they assured Charity, was large and modern and cheerful. "You could perhaps try your luck, Charity?"

It was the Outpatients Sister who spoke as they sat drinking their coffee. "With our professor, you know—you see him a great deal and you are not like us." Her eyes flickered to Charity's splendid hair, "You are new and you do not speak Dutch, which makes you interesting."

Charity put her cup down carefully and said just as carefully: "Well, you see I'm not a fast worker and I'll be gone again quite soon, I think. Besides..."

"A boy in England?" asked Tina quickly.

It was an easy way out of a conversation she wasn't much enjoying.

"Yes."

"But, of course," said someone, "Charity is pretty, she is already engaged, perhaps?"

"We shall be when I get back to England," stated Charity firmly, and actually believed what she said.

After that day she had her off duty like everyone else, only Zuster Doelsma begged her to forfeit her days off. "If you would not mind too much?" she asked. "I am sure that once you are back in den Haag, they will certainly be made up to you." She paused. "You see, your Mr Boekerchek is sometimes a little difficult with my nurses and not so very easy to understand—and he is a private patient..." She didn't finish the sentence and Charity said at once, understanding her very well: "Of course I don't mind—I couldn't do much anyway, for I don't know my way around. I'm perfectly happy with my free afternoons and that seems to suit everyone, doesn't it?"

So every day, when she had settled her patient for

his post-prandial nap, she went out, sometimes with Sisters who were off duty too, sometimes on her own. There was plenty to engage her interest; she visited museums and churches and wandered the streets, and then went back and gave Mr Boekerchek her impressions of what she had seen while she prepared him for bed.

Professor van Tijlen only came once a day now, in the mornings, and beyond asking her in a civil way if she was satisfied with everything, had nothing more to say. He had become a little remote, she discovered, though he had never been over-friendly in the first place. All the same she had to admit that he was nice to work for; her quick mind understood his directions almost before he had said them, and they saw eye to eye in all matters concerning the patient. Indeed, she found herself looking forward to his visits, telling herself it was because she admired and respected him for his work, whatever her opinion of him as a man might be—which was a point she took care not to pursue.

Mr Boekerchek was to go home in five days' time; he had made a splendid recovery and had responded satisfactorily to all the tests done upon him, although the professor had frowned thoughtfully when Charity reported the occasional headaches the American still had.

"I hope," he told her, "that there is to be no recurrence of the insulinomata—there was no sign of another when I operated. You will be good enough to let me know if any of the symptoms, however slight, should return. I understand that you are to stay in den Haag for a further two weeks.''

So he didn't intend to visit Mr Boekerchek there. She felt a strong urge to see more of him, if only to turn his attention from the pretty fair-haired girl in his car, a wish she recognised as childish in the extreme, but the chance was unlikely.

But not too unlikely, as it turned out; she met him the very next afternoon. It was a glorious day and she had put on a white sleeveless dress, green sandals, and slung a matching shoulder bag on her arm and gone off to explore on her own. The whole afternoon was before her; she stood on the edge of the pavement, trying to decide if she could stroll round viewing the city or go to yet another museum.

Her mind was made up for her by the professor, who appeared suddenly and without fussy comment at her side. ''Going somewhere particular?'' he wanted to know.

''No—I was just deciding…''

''In that case, allow me to show you a little of Holland.''

His car was at the kerb although she hadn't noticed it. She found herself sitting beside him as he drove through the busy streets, without quite knowing how it had happened.

''Well, really,'' she began, ''did I say I'd come with you?''

He laughed. "No—surprise is a good tactic, is it not?"

"Yes—well, it's very kind of you, but I have to be back on duty at half past five."

"And it is now two o'clock. Time enough and to spare."

They were out of the city now, tearing along the motorway, but presently when they reached a village, he turned off into a narrow country road.

"The river Vecht," explained the professor, "noted for the houses built along its banks. The rich merchants built them during the eighteenth century and they are still inhabited by members of their families. A friend of mine who works at the hospital—Max Oosterwelde—lives in one of them. He's married to an English girl, by the way. The river is enchanting, is it not, and the houses decidedly picturesque."

He was right, on such a day they could be nothing else. There was little traffic on the road and the shining little river with the nice old houses crowding its banks appeared the epitome of peace. Charity sighed with content.

"It's beautiful," she agreed fervently. "It must be nice living here."

"Very convenient for Utrecht," her companion pointed out, "though at weekends and during the holiday period it can get crowded. It's a show-place."

They had reached a fork in the road, and he took the right-hand one.

"The village of Loenen," he told her, "a great sailing centre. We'll have tea."

They had their tea at a charming café by the water's edge while the professor discoursed about his country. "A pity you are not here for a longer stay," he remarked casually, "but of course you want to get back to England as soon as possible. I am told that you are intending to marry."

She might have known that Dutch hospitals had grapevines as well as their English counterparts. She said a trifle tartly: "I shouldn't have thought that you would have listened to gossip, Professor."

His straight brows rose slightly. "Gossip? My dear good girl, I take a fatherly interest in the nurses who work for me."

He didn't look in the least fatherly; he looked shockingly handsome, very sure of himself, and slightly amused. Charity's tongue spoke the words she had thought but never intended to voice. "You didn't look in the least fatherly the other evening."

Her green eyes sparkled with rising temper, not improved at all by his laugh. "I'm flattered that you were sufficiently interested to notice us," he said smoothly, "but I must point out that I said that I was fatherly towards my nurses."

She bit savagely into a sandwich. If that wasn't a

snub, she would like to know what was. "I am not in the least interested," she began haughtily.

"A pity," he was smiling faintly. "Try one of these little cakes, I can recommend them."

Charity took one, feeling awkward. Presently she spoke with the air of someone maintaining the social graces at all costs. "Do you come here often?"

A silly remark, she realised too late. For: "Indeed I do—it is one of my favourite places to which I bring my girl-friends," he answered in a silky voice.

Unanswerable. "Would you like some more tea?" she asked stiffly, and took a long time filling his cup while she tried to think of something to talk about.

"Mr Boekerchek is doing very nicely," she remarked brightly as she passed the cup back again, only to be squashed by his: "I never discuss my patients when I'm off duty, dear girl."

"I'm not your dear girl," she snapped.

"Not at the moment," he agreed placidly, and just as though he were being the pleasantest of companions: "I like your name, although it is a little unusual. Are you called Charity by your family?"

His voice was friendly and almost soothing, she felt her temper improving as she told him that no, she was called Cherry at home, and when he asked where home was, she told him that too, and about her parents and Lucy who wanted to marry the doctor's son and her brother in the Army and married. She stopped presently with the nasty suspicion that she was talking too much. "How I do run on," she observed apologetically. "I'm sorry, it's so boring for you."

"I'm not bored. I thought your parents looked delightful, even though your father seemed annoyed."

She eyed him in astonishment. "But how did you know which car...?"

"My dear Charity, I may be middle-aged, but I still have the use of my faculties."

She said quickly: "You're not middle-aged—what utter nonsense!"

They were getting up to go. "How kind," he drawled. "I must invite you out again, you're good for my self-esteem."

He smiled mockingly as he spoke and she could think of nothing to say.

She saw him only once more to speak to, other than the brief words which passed between them concerning the patient. It was her last evening in the hospital; they were to leave in the morning, travelling by car this time. Charity had made everything ready for their departure, made her own farewells and acted as dispenser of coffee, general messenger, and anything else Mr Boekerchek, cock-a-hoop at being fully alive again, had chosen to think up for her. She felt tired and dispirited although she had no reason to be; it had been a happy day; Mr Boekerchek had handed out parting gifts with the lavishness of Father Christmas, and there had been a constant stream of visitors to his room. None of these things had worried her, she was just as happy as anyone else that her patient was well—or almost so—again, it was something which he had said which had clung so persistently to her thoughts.

The professor had promised to look in that evening, and hours before then Mr Boekerchek had shown her a handsome silver salver, suitably engraved, which he intended to give his surgeon. "A little extra something," he had explained to her, "for he's a mighty clever man, is Professor van Tijlen, and worth every gulden of his fee." And he had mentioned a sum of such magnitude that Charity had uttered a surprised "oh" of astonishment; that the professor deserved to be well paid for his work she would have been the last to deny, but his fee was surely very high—no wonder he could indulge himself with expensive cars, beautifully cut suits and silk shirts—probably he lived in one of those modern penthouses and changed the revolting *avant-garde* furniture several times a year; and possibly, she thought waspishly, the beautiful fair-haired girl had her pickings, too. For some reason the very thought put her out of temper, so that when she came face to face with him in the corridor, she made no attempt to take the scowl off her pretty face, framed as it was in a veritable bower of hothouse flowers her patient had bidden her take over to the Nurses' Home. The professor stopped as he drew abreast of her.

"Ah, Miss Dawson," he uttered suavely, "bearing away the spoils of victory?"

This remark, coming as it did hard on her reflections concerning his fee, was sufficient for her to send discretion to the four winds and give vent to her feelings.

"A remark more appropriate to yourself, Professor," she declared fierily, her fine eyes flashing.

He stood looking down at her, his hands in the pockets of one of the exquisite suits she had been thinking about. "Do explain," he invited her, and smiled a little.

She mistrusted the smile and she certainly had no business talking to a senior member of the hospital staff in such a manner, but it was too late to have cold feet about it now and she wasn't going to apologise.

With only the faintest shake in her voice she said: "Mr Boekerchek told me how much your fees were." She paused; his expression hadn't altered at all. She wondered briefly what he was thinking behind that calm face and went doggedly on: "I think it was a great deal of money." She gulped. "Too much."

He still looked calm. Charity peered out from the tastefully arranged bouquets of roses and carnations and fern, and clutched them desperately, wishing he would speak. When he did, his voice was so soft that she could scarcely hear it.

"The devil you do, Miss Dawson," he remarked,

and sounded the very soul of good nature, "but you forget my expensive tastes, do you not?—my cars, my girl-friends—for all you know, I drink champagne with every meal. A man must live, dear girl, something I suspect you have not yet begun to do."

Her mouth opened in a regrettable gape, but no sound came from it; she had expected anger, a demand for an apology, even summary dismissal, but not this quiet voice like steel. She managed at last: "Oh, I do beg your pardon, I had no right—I must have been mad." And then, because she was an honest girl: "But I meant what I said."

He was staring at her very hard; she thought that he was going to say something, but he didn't, only smiled, unexpectedly and with great sweetness, and went on his way, whistling softly.

They left the next morning in a good deal of pomp, in the Embassy car and with a chauffeur to carry the remaining flowers and Mr Boekerchek's personal treasures, and Mrs Boekerchek, wringing everyone by the hand twice over. They were seen off by a great many people too, but the professor wasn't there. Charity, who had been nervous of meeting him again, told herself that it was a good thing he wasn't, for it would have been a little awkward. Besides, she reminded herself even while she searched the people around them in case he had come at the last moment, she had no wish to see him again. She had been interested in him; now she wasn't any more. By a great

effort of will she managed not to look back as they
drove away from the hospital; he could have been at
one of the windows.

The apartment in den Haag seemed very quiet and
a little dull after hospital life. True, she had the delightful bedroom again and every conceivable comfort
and not a great deal to do. Dr Donker called each
day, chatted with the patient, looked at her carefully
kept charts, enquired as to symptoms, and went on
his way again, leaving her to coax her patient to take
sufficient rest between the constant stream of callers.
He was up for most of the day now, pottering around
the apartment and taking gentle little strolls in the
Haagsche Bos, driven there in the Cadillac. Charity
went with him, of course, for there was little else for
her to do; there were still tests to be made at regular
intervals, but his progress was steady, and she wasn't
surprised when he told her, with genuine regret, that
she might make arrangements to return to St Simon's.
"But not until after Saturday," he urged her. "There
is to be a little party at the Embassy and you are
invited—besides, I should like you to be there, it'll
be my first real outing and I reckon I'm nervous."

So she wrote to Miss Evans, saying that she would
be returning on the following Sunday, and went along
to Mrs Boekerchek's little sitting-room to discuss the
important topic of what to wear. It was only Tuesday,
so she had time enough to buy something; she had
explored the city during her free time and she knew

which shops to go to and, because she had had very little chance to spend it, a moderately full purse.

Full evening dress, Mrs Boekerchek had told her, and led her to her bedroom to exhibit the grey embroidered lace she had bought specially for the occasion. "It's not a very large party," she explained, "a hundred or so, and it's always the same people, you know—but it's really a celebration of Arthur's recovery." She broke off to ask anxiously: "He'll be OK, won't he, honey—I'm so nervous."

"You don't need to be," Charity assured her, "and I promise you that I'll keep an eye on him and if I see he's getting tired, I'll let you know at once, and you can persuade him to come home."

Mrs Boekerchek beamed at her. "I don't know how we'll get on without you, Charity—or that nice professor. Doesn't it strike you as providential that Arthur should have met you both like that the very first time he was ill, and it was the pair of you who got him well again?" She looked kindly at Charity. "You don't hear from him?—the professor, I mean."

Charity shook her head and made her voice matter-of-fact. "No, Mrs Boekerchek, and I don't expect to. Any number of nurses work for him, you see, and consultants don't notice us as people, really—just nurses to do what is required for the patient's good."

"It doesn't seem right, somehow," said her companion vaguely, and when Charity could find nothing to say to this, asked if she intended buying a new dress.

Charity went shopping the very next afternoon and found just what she wanted at the Galeries Modernes, although the price was an extravagant one. A long white dress, full-skirted and long-sleeved, with a high, demure neckline. It was collared and cuffed with lace threaded with aquamarine ribbons with a sash of the same colour, and quite carried away by its charm, she matched this confection with satin slippers. She bore her purchases home in triumph and tried them on under Mrs Boekerchek's motherly eye and received her heartfelt admiration. "Just the thing for your hair," said that lady generously. "I reckon you'll be a success, Charity; the men will be so glad to see a new face." She added, "And such a pretty one, too."

The rest of the week passed too quickly. Charity had seen almost nothing of Holland, save for that one short outing with the professor, and there wasn't sufficient time to explore den Haag during her free afternoons, for she needed that to buy presents to take home. Mr Boekerchek was depending less and less on her, too, although he enjoyed her company when he took his exercise. He was going back to his office in a few weeks after he and his wife had been on holiday. The whole episode was almost closed; she would go back to St Simon's and take up the reins of management once more and after a little while she would have difficulty in remembering anything about her visit to Holland. That this assumption bore no resemblance to the truth she refused to admit, even to herself. She pushed the thought to the back of her head, and concentrated deliberately on Saturday's junketings.

They arrived a little late at the Embassy, for Mr Boekerchek had dozed off after his tea and Charity had been reluctant to wake him, so that the evening was in full swing by the time they arrived. To Charity, standing in the imposing entrance hall, waiting for Mrs Boekerchek to return from the urgent rearrangement of her hair, the affair seemed more like a reception than a party, for the gentlemen were resplendent in white ties and tails, and the ladies were in long dresses. She was thankful that she had bought a new dress for such a grand occasion and that it was so entirely suitable. True, a few pearls or a diamond piece would have been nice to adorn her person; most of the women had a great many jewels, and she had nothing at all. But the dress was pretty, she assured herself as at last Mrs Boekerchek rejoined them and they started up the stairs.

It was gratifying to find, after half an hour or so, that she wasn't going to lack partners for the evening. She was quickly surrounded by a cluster of gentlemen from the various Embassies, anxious to make her acquaintance and dance with her. Indeed, she could have spent the entire evening on the dance floor, but

mindful of her patient, she took care to sit with him
from time to time and make certain that he wasn't
exerting himself unduly. Only when she saw him
nicely settled with two elderly gentlemen with strong
mid-European accents did she return to the dance
floor, escorted by a young and still obscure secretary
from the German Embassy, who unlike Professor van
Tijlen, encouraged her to air her German, so that it
was with some discomfort that she became aware that
the professor was standing at her elbow. The sight of
him, quite unexpected, made her break off in mid-
sentence hashing her Teutonic grammar hopelessly
and causing her to greet him with understandable
coldness.

Apparently he had forgotten their last meeting, for
he wished her and her companion an affable good
evening and went on blandly:

"Don't let me interrupt you in your exercise of the
German tongue, Miss Dawson. I can't say that you
have made much progress, but enthusiasm is the great
thing, is it not?" He turned to the other man and
spoke to him in a German which shamed her own and
which she didn't quite catch, and rather to her surprise, Herr Schmidt begged her to excuse him and
walked rapidly away.

"Well," exclaimed Charity, "whatever did you
say to him?" and when the professor only smiled, she
went on: "And there was no need for you to show
off like that. I cannot think why you should be so

amused when I choose to speak another language than my own. And now if you will excuse me…''

''No, I won't.'' He laid a large gentle hand on her arm. ''Tell me, have you learned any Dutch yet?''

Her eyes flashed greenly. ''No, and I don't intend to.'' She spoke with some spirit, disregarding entirely the fact that she had learned quite a fair amount of the language during the last week or so. ''And kindly let go of my arm.''

''No.'' He was smiling again. ''Tell me, do you still hold me in contempt?''

She was too surprised to answer him, only after a stunned moment she shook her head and presently she mumbled: ''I don't suppose it is of the least importance to you what I should think.''

He laughed at that and she went on crossly: ''I'm sure you find it all very amusing.'' A feeling she wasn't sharing, indeed, she felt a strong desire to burst into tears, which in the light of the evening's pleasures was absurd.

''You look as though you're going to cry,'' observed her companion conversationally.

She blinked rapidly with her fantastic eyelashes. ''Professor van Tijlen,'' she uttered in a low, furious voice, quite forgetting the awful things she had said to him about his fees, ''I hope you will believe me when I say that I dislike you more than anyone else I know.''

His grey eyes swept her face. ''No, I don't believe

you, but being nicely brought up, I know when to make myself scarce." His eyes left her face and he glanced round the room; almost immediately they were joined by an elderly bearded man whom the professor introduced as "My uncle, Mijnheer van Tijlen, from the Dutch Embassy," who professed himself delighted at making her acquaintance and began at once to talk about England, a country, he assured her, of which he was very fond. He had barely begun a dissertation on Stonehenge, which he had recently visited, when his nephew excused himself.

Charity didn't speak to him for the rest of the evening, which had unaccountably become deadly dull. She watched him dancing with a succession of ladies, with each of whom he appeared to be on the friendliest terms, and when, during an old-fashioned waltz, she found herself, partnered by a cheerful young man from the French Embassy, in such close proximity to the professor and his partner that she was able to overhear him expressing the warmest admiration for that lady's dress, she smouldered with vexation; he had made no remark at all about her own appearance, and as each successive partner had been eager to tell her how very pretty her gown was, she was forced to the conclusion that either his taste in women's clothes was poor, or that he just hadn't noticed what she was wearing. Neither of these surmises cheered her in the least, and when Mr Boekerchek decided that he wished to leave the party, she was the first to urge him to do so, and even though the professor came over to say goodnight to his patient and his wife, he did no more than accord her a cool, "Goodbye, Miss Dawson."

Getting into the car to go back to the apartment, Charity remembered that she wouldn't see him again; this tiresome thought persisted until long after she was in bed. She should have gone to sleep immediately after such an exciting evening; she did no such thing, however, but lay frowning into the dark, alternately disliking the professor very much and then finding all kinds of excuses for him. Just before she at last slept she admitted to herself that she had been appallingly rude and probably he had resented it very much—she would have resented such remarks herself—they had been almost slanderous, or did she mean libellous? She was still deciding in a muddle-headed way when she fell asleep.

CHAPTER FOUR

CHARITY HAD BEEN back five days and had hated every moment of each one of them. The ward was busy enough; her staff were delighted to have her back, and those of the patients who were still in the ward expressed their pleasure at seeing her again, too. Yet the effort to be cheerful and patient with everyone was a big one, and although she maintained her professionally bright face when she was on duty, off duty she was inclined to sit staring at nothing, so that her closer friends asked her if she had quarrelled with Clive.

He was away on a short holiday and she had hardly noticed it; she assured those who asked that there had been no quarrel and that she was looking forward to seeing him when he returned—indeed, she imagined that it was his absence that made her feel so low in spirits. That and the absence of Mr Howard; perhaps when they both came back she would feel herself again.

Clive returned first. She met him on the ward, doing his usual round before noon, and was at once struck by his air of constraint. She accompanied him as usual, and as usual invited him to have coffee with her afterwards, but he pleaded an appointment for which he was already late and said he would see her later. Charity watched his departing back, a little puzzled; perhaps he was feeling awkward because she hadn't said if she would marry him yet; she realised with a guilty pang that she hadn't written to him while she had been in Holland, so very likely he was hurt and upset about her neglect.

She went into her office and poured out her coffee and then sat watching it get cold while she thought. The future looked, for some reason, uninviting, probably because she hadn't made up her mind about Clive. Perhaps it would be the right thing to marry him after all; she liked him enormously, they didn't get on each other's nerves, and they had similar tastes—besides, being a nurse, she had a very good idea of what would be expected of her when they married and she would be able to help him a good deal.

When he returned to the ward that afternoon and asked her, still with that air of constraint, if she would go out with him that evening, she accepted readily. He would probably propose again and this time she would say yes.

She was late off duty; a last-minute emergency had held her up. She changed into the first dress which came to hand and skimped her make-up, conscious that she wasn't looking her best. But Clive had seen her looking far worse; Charity swept her hair up into a bun and raced downstairs.

She didn't ask where they were going, taking it for granted that it would be their usual restaurant, as indeed it was. They were on the point of going in when Clive, who had been unusually silent, said:

"I thought it would be fun to make up a little party—you have already met."

They had indeed. Margery was looking prettier than ever and even more helpless in a pale blue dress which exactly matched her eyes. It took only a few moments for Charity to discover that Margery's father took it for granted that she had come along for his entertainment; he took her arm and led her to a table in the window, leaving the other two to follow. "Let them have a minute or two to themselves," he suggested in a conspiratorial manner. "I've a soft spot for young people in love."

Charity allowed herself to be seated. Amazement had bereft her of words, and hard on the heels of amazement came relief; she hadn't wanted to marry Clive at all. Seeing him there, mooning over Margery, made him seem so young…she caught his eye and smiled quite gaily at him. He looked positively hang-dog until she said brightly: "I knew this was going to happen, but I can't think why you didn't write and tell me."

"You don't mind?" Margery asked warily.

"Why ever should I? Clive and I have always been

good friends, and always will be, I hope, and now we two can be good friends as well. When is the wedding to be?''

They told her, both talking at once, obviously relieved that the situation had been carried off in such a friendly fashion, and all she needed to do was to acclaim their plans with enthusiasm and turn a polite ear to the old man's plans for his son-in-law's future. It was all very cosy and chatty and the conversation had as much sparkle as a wet Monday morning, thought Charity peevishly. It was a pity that Clive hadn't plucked up the courage to tell her that morning and then she need not have come. Had he been frightened of her?

The thought that perhaps he was and always had been, just a little, crossed her mind as she talked and laughed and joined in the inevitable toasts, and she mused a little bitterly on the fact that being a good looking and intelligent girl wasn't any help at all if all the men she met were going to be timid of her. If she had had a boastful disposition, trying to impress everyone she met, it would have served her right, but she had done her best to conceal her brains, and her looks she couldn't help, anyway.

So for Charity the evening wasn't all that of a success; by the time she had been deposited at St Simon's door she had a raging headache and a very uncertain temper, and although the headache was better by the morning, her temper wasn't. She concealed it well, she considered, but Mr Howard, back from his holiday and rather terse in consequence, wanted to know what had bitten her.

"Frustrated," he told her, "that's what you are. Locked in that starched apron and longing to tear it off. What's the matter? Didn't you enjoy your trip to Holland?"

She assured him politely that she had and chose to ignore the first of his remarks.

"What's the matter, then?" he persisted. "Fallen in love with Everard?"

She went a little pale but asked gamely: "Who is Everard?"

"Professor van Tijlen, if we're going to be formal about it. Nice chap, wish I had his brains—and his looks, for that matter. Gave you his article to read, didn't I?"

"Yes, you did. I found it most useful—the case was very interesting."

Mr Howard gave her a searching look, said gruffly: "Yes, well—I must move on to the children's ward, I suppose," and stalked away.

Charity, left on her own, started to go back to the ward and then changed her mind and went into her office instead and sat down at her desk. She was feeling a little peculiar; she had known it all the time, she supposed, and hadn't been prepared to admit it. It had taken Mr Howard's question to unwrap the fact that she was in love with Professor van Tijlen, and now that she allowed herself to admit it she might just as well be honest—she had been in love with him since the moment she had set eyes on him. Full stop. For everything was finished and done with; he would have forgotten her already and now she would have to forget him, something which was going to take all her determination.

She went back into the ward, a little pale still and went through the rest of the day, true to her resolution, not thinking about him at all—or only when she couldn't prevent herself, but she thought about a great many other things; that evening when she got off duty she wrote out her resignation.

It created quite a stir for the logical conclusion which everyone drew was that Clive had jilted her, or, more probably, she had refused to marry him. Neither surmise worried her; she was leaving for a sufficiently good reason; a new job in a new place would fill her mind with other thoughts and in time, it was to be hoped, blot them out entirely. In the meantime, she talked to Clive, was careful to be seen with him, maintain her friendliness towards him and even join him and Margery on an evening's outing, so that after a few days of wild rumours the hospital was forced to the conclusion that nothing outstanding had happened or was going to happen. Her story that she felt that she needed a change was accepted by all but the most sceptical, and in due course she was sped on her way, burdened by a variety of farewell gifts and with a homily from Miss Evans still ringing in her ears. She had been very foolish, that lady had told her sternly, to give up a good position for no valid reason. She had paused expectantly here, in the hope that Charity might supply the reason, but she remained silent, which gave Miss Evans the opportunity of telling her that she had always known that the journey to Holland had been a mistake. A change of mind which Charity might have argued about. But there seemed no point in it; Miss Evans had never liked her over much; probably she was glad to see her go and Staff Gay already in her shoes. They wished each other a coldly polite goodbye and Charity got into her car and drove home, her mind empty of plans for the future. That there would have to be plans before very long she was well aware, but she would have a week or two at home first. After all, she told herself, when one broke an arm or a leg, one had a period of convalescence while it mended. Surely a broken heart merited the same treatment?

The quiet peace of home was wonderful to her. No one questioned her decision to leave St Simon's, there was plenty of room in the house for her, Lucy was delighted to have her home for a while and her mother and father absorbed her into their lives as though she had never been away. She tramped for miles with the dogs, gardened with her father and drove her mother down to Budleigh Salterton to shop and visit her friends. Her days were healthily full; she should have bloomed in the air and the sun instead of becoming thinner and paler.

Her father, worried at the dark shadows under her eyes, gave her a glass of his best port each morning, wearing that she had become run down and had worked too hard. Her mother said nothing at all, and because she never mentioned Holland, no one else did. Only one morning when she received a letter from Mr Boekerchek did her mother remark that it was nice not to lose contact with people—a vague remark which needed no reply.

Charity had been home two weeks or more when her father was stricken with a touch of lumbago just as the early potatoes needed digging. Lucy was use-less with a spade, there was no question of her mother attempting such work. Charity, glad of something to do, put on a pair of old slacks and a cotton shirt which had seen better days, and repaired to the kitchen gar-den. It was the best part of her father's modest grounds, up on the hill behind the house, with a view of the sea through the trees and the great sweep of Woodbury Common at its back. Even early in the morning it was warm work but rewarding; she had several piles of potatoes to show for her labours when she heard footsteps coming along the path from the house. Without looking round she called: "There's no need for you to come; I'm doing very well—I'll be down in a half hour or so. You shouldn't be here, you know.''

She was kneeling on the warm earth, grubbing the potatoes out with her hands. She dropped the handful she was holding when she was plucked from the ground, stood on her feet, and turned round.

''I shouldn't be here—you are quite right,'' Professor van Tijlen observed with all the casualness of one who had seen her not five minutes earlier instead of five weeks or more, ''but there is a need.''

He stared down at her, still holding her firmly in an impersonal grasp. ''I'm not here on my own behalf—that would be unlikely, would it not? but our Mr Arthur C. Boekerchek is very ill again. I shall have to do an exploration and he flatly refuses to have it done unless he can have you back again as his nurse. There is not a day to lose, so I came over myself to ask you.'' His grey eyes searched her face. ''That hatchet-faced virago at Simon's told me that you had left and she wasn't disposed to give me your address—however, I persuaded her.''

He sounded rather grim and Charity spared a few seconds from her own bewildered thoughts to wonder how he had persuaded anyone as formidable as Miss Evans to do anything she didn't wish to. She was brought back to the amazing present by his remark: ''I want to operate on Thursday.''

She found her voice at last. ''But it's Tuesday already, and you're here.''

"We can be away in an hour—I hadn't reckoned on you not being in London but we can still be back in Utrecht by tomorrow night."

The enchantment of seeing him again had emptied her head of all her usual common sense. With a great effort she made herself think.

"It's what? half past nine? Will you go over on the evening ferry?" And when he nodded: "So we should have to leave here by midday—that's if you've got the Lamborghini..." He nodded again, not interrupting her. "So there's about two hours." She stared down at her earthy hands, dusting them off. "Yes, Professor, of course I'll come. I'll go and change and pack now. Will you come to the house—I'll get some coffee."

She was already leading the way down the path, but stopped to look at him. "Have you slept at all? would you like...?"

He smiled faintly as he interrupted her. "You're kind—but then Charity is kind, is she not? Yes, I have had all the sleep I need, but I should love some coffee."

"And sandwiches," she added as they went in through the back door. "If we eat something before we go, it won't matter if there's no time to stop on the way."

In the kitchen she found Lucy already busy and her mother, surprisingly calm about their unexpected visitor, getting a tray of coffee ready. They had introduced themselves, she told Charity with a smile for the professor, and perhaps he would like to go and talk to her father while she had a bath and got some clothes together. ''And I'll be up in a minute to help you pack, dear,'' called her parent as she went up-stairs.

She was downstairs again within half an hour, still not quite believing that the man she had been trying to forget was sitting opposite her father, discussing the growing of roses. Seeing him there, stretched out comfortably in the old-fashioned armchair, she wondered how she could have been silly enough to suppose that she could ever forget him. She never would, she knew that now, nor would she be able to tell him that she had lied when she had told him that she disliked him—not that that mattered, for he so obviously didn't mind what she thought of him—she had made no impression upon him at all, but she happened to be a good nurse and he required her services; his personal feelings didn't enter into it.

He got up as she went into the sitting-room, pulled forward a chair for her and then resumed his talk with her father. In the strong light of the summer morning she could see that he was tired and the strong sunshine turning the grey in his hair to silver made him seem more so. Following her train of thought she asked: ''Would you like me to drive for the first part of the trip?'' and could have bitten out her tongue the moment she had said it; he would laugh, of course, or at best refuse; he might even make some remark about women drivers, although she thought it unlikely. He did none of these things, but accepted her offer promptly without any show of surprise, and her father broke off his earnest advice about black spot long enough to observe: "Oh, Cherry's a born driver—you'll be quite safe with her."

She was a little nervous of the Lamborghini to begin with, but as its owner, sitting beside her, showed no signs of anxiety, the enjoyment of driving such a splendid car overcame her nerves. Safely over Woodbury Common and through Honiton, she relaxed a little. They hadn't talked much; casual remarks about the weather and the scenery, no more, and after a silence lasting rather longer than before, she asked him where he wanted to take over the driving. When he didn't reply she ventured a quick look. The professor was asleep. She drove on, her feelings alternating between pleasure at his faith in her driving and vexation at his complete lack of interest in herself.

She was too good a driver to allow her thoughts to colour her driving; all the same, two hours later with the M3 within striking distance, the vexation was rapidly getting the upper hand.

"Pull into the next lay-by," suggested her companion gently, "and we'll change places."

The suspicion that he hadn't been asleep at all crossed her mind as she did as he had suggested and brought the car to a halt before she turned to look at him. "Why did you pretend to be asleep?" she asked sharply, certain that her guess was correct.

"Oh, but I did sleep for quite half an hour," he gave her an innocent look which she didn't trust, "and you were driving so well it seemed a good idea not to distract your attention from the road. Besides, I had some thinking to do."

Charity looked down her lovely nose; if he preferred thinking to engaging her in conversation, then she couldn't care less, she told herself as they changed places, and when he asked her if she was quite comfortable, she answered him with a decided snap and turned her head away to watch the countryside. She kept it there for a long time and only turned it back again because she had such a crick in the neck.

"Ah," said Professor van Tijlen instantly, "out of the sulks?"

He was driving at a steady seventy now, with all the nonchalance of a boy on a bicycle, but not, she was bound to admit, putting a foot wrong. She choked on the torrent of words which crowded her tongue and managed a calm: "I'm not sulking; I have no reason to do so."

"Liar," he said cheerfully. "I've yet to meet a pretty girl who didn't expect a large slice of attention from her men companions—and turned sour when she didn't get it."

Charity smouldered for several seconds and when she spoke her voice was high with temper. "You are a very rude man, the rudest I have had the misfortune to meet! I can't think why I agreed to come back with you to Holland—indeed, it's only because Mr Boekerchek wants me—for two pins you can stop the car and I'll go back home!''

''For such an experienced driver you're singularly ignorant of the rules of the road, dear girl. We are on a motorway, remember? Besides, I should be endangering both your life and your limbs if I were to dump you in the middle of the M3.'' His voice changed and became gentle and friendly. ''I don't mean to tease. I'll apologise handsomely, shall I? And for good measure I'll give you full marks for being such a good driver—there aren't many I would trust myself to in my own car.''

The unqualified generosity of this pronouncement caused her to forget her ill humour and exclaim: ''Oh, do you really mean that?''

''Indeed I do.'' He spoilt it by adding, ''If only your accent were as faultless as your driving.''

He seemed determined to annoy her, and Charity wondered, rather unhappily, why. She said with surprising meekness: ''I don't have much opportunity of speaking any language but my own.''

He glanced sideways at her. ''I hear that you are a very clever young woman.''

She answered him seriously, without conceit, thinking of Clive.

''It's a great handicap. I should like to be small

and fair and too delicate to lift things..." She broke off at his roar of laughter and said huffily: "It's all very well to laugh, you're not a girl."

Which made him laugh still more.

They were almost at Camberley and she wondered which way he intended going; they hadn't stopped at all and they had been travelling more than three hours. As though he had read her thoughts, he said: "I'm going to turn off here and cut across to Maidstone—we can pick up the M2 on the other side. We'll stop for lunch."

She imagined that they would stop somewhere along the road, but he travelled on until they had almost reached Reigate, when he turned off again, so that she asked a little anxiously: "Is there time? I mean, we're off the road."

"Plenty of time—and we need a little peace and quiet for half an hour, don't you agree?"

He stopped in Abinger and took her to a quiet little country pub, where the food was surprisingly good. She hadn't realised how hungry she was, and now she thought about it, tired too, so that she was grateful for her companion's casual conversation which required little or no effort on her part. He was being very nice; she supposed that he would be nice to anyone in similar circumstances, whether he liked them or not; he was good at hiding his feelings and she was, after all, a guest, more or less, until she reached the hospital, and he was a man who would accord his guest every courtesy, even if he detested them. The thought was a lowering one.

He hadn't mentioned his patient once; presumably he would tell her all she needed to know when they arrived at the hospital.

"I've no uniform," she exclaimed suddenly.

They had had their coffee and were sitting at their leisure, facing each other across the small table. "They'll fix you up at the hospital," he assured her confidently, "there must be someone there who is your size."

She choked. "I should hope so. I'm quite a normal shape, you know."

He twinkled nicely at her and she thought he was going to say something quite different from his: "Did I imply that you weren't? I'm sorry. Shall we go?"

For the rest of their journey the professor maintained a pleasant, impersonal manner towards her— he was consideration itself when it came to her comfort, but he showed no sign of wanting to get to know her better. His conversation was casual and did not touch once upon herself or anything to do with her, nor did he exhibit any curiosity as to her reasons for leaving St Simon's, or her plans for the future. Which was a good thing, for she had none.

The ferry was tolerably full, the evening pleasant. They had stopped for a cup of tea before they went on board and once there, Charity politely refused the professor's offer of a meal in the ship's restaurant, largely because he so obviously had expected her to accept his invitation, but she had cause to regret this an hour or so later for she had a healthy appetite and she was hungry. But by this time her companion had opened his despatch case and was immersed in its contents, making notes in his spidery scribble, oblivious of his surroundings. She leafed through the generous pile of magazines he had bought for her and thought longingly of food while she studied him covertly.

He was a handsome man, there was no doubt of that, but she thought it unlikely that he allowed that fact to concern him overmuch; he was self-assured, true, but not self-conscious. She was contemplating his high-bridged nose when he looked up and caught her at it. She saw the muscle twitch at the side of his mouth and went a delicate pink, but all he said was "How about a sandwich?"

She thanked him in a relieved voice which caused the muscle to twitch again as he went in search of refreshment. He came back very shortly with a tray loaded down with cups of tea and a variety of sandwiches, and while she ate the simple meal she watched him working his way through the sandwiches like a hungry schoolboy while he explained that he was making notes for a lecture he had been asked to give in Vienna shortly.

"You don't mind if I work?" he asked her somewhat belatedly. "It's a splendid opportunity, for I am not distracted by anybody.'' He smiled in a kindly fashion at her; quite obviously there was nothing about her person to distract him. Not that she would wish that, she reminded herself sternly, she wasn't in the least interested in him or the things he did or the way he lived, even though she loved him—a highly satisfactory state of affairs which didn't prevent her from falling into a brown study as to where he lived and what his home was like and who looked after him.

He went back to his writing presently and she gave a good imitation of reading *Vogue*. They didn't speak again until he gathered up his papers at last and remarked that they should be almost there. Which they were.

They had about a hundred miles to go, through Antwerp and on to the motorway to Breda and Utrecht. Charity had never been that way before, and she found the country flat and depressing; she was feeling tired now and was secretly thankful that she would have a little time to get settled in before the operation. Her companion talked seldom; she supposed that he had a lot on his mind and as they understood each other so well, he had no need to exert himself to be charming; she had told him that she didn't like him. She frowned; it was a pity that she couldn't tell him the truth, but that of course wouldn't do.

Their journey was almost over. It was half past eleven at night, she swallowed a yawn and hoped he hadn't noticed. It would be nice to lean her sleepy head on his enormous shoulder, but it might interfere with his driving—beside, it was the wrong head; she wasn't the pretty fair-haired girl who had been in the car with him.

The hospital lay silent, most of its windows dark, only here and there did she glimpse the faint night lights in the wards. The professor stopped the car outside the main entrance, warned the night porter to let the Night Superintendent know that they had arrived, and took her luggage from the boot.

Charity watched him, a disappointment she didn't understand filling her tired senses. It caused her to say quite tartly: "Please don't wait, I'm perfectly able to find my way—you must want to get home."

To which speech he answered nothing at all. When the Night Superintendent arrived, the professor engaged her in conversation for a few moments, told the porter to find someone to take the luggage over to the Home, and then asked Zuster Wit if she would be good enough to let his registrar know that he was back. Only when both these persons had gone on their errands did he turn to Charity. She couldn't see him very clearly in the dim light of the entrance hall and when he took a step towards her, she asked: "Did you want something?"

"Yes, this," he said softly, and bent to kiss her. She was still finding her breath when he said on a half laugh: "Kiss and be friends—is that not what you say in your country?"

He took her by the shoulders and gave her a gentle push. "Now go to bed, Miss Dawson."

CHAPTER FIVE

MR BOEKERCHEK was in the same room as he had previously and he certainly looked ill, although his face lighted up when he saw Charity and he broke at once into a string of apologies for bringing her all the way back to Holland. "But I couldn't face it all over again, honey, not unless you were there to bully me and make me laugh and stop me being scared." He peered at her anxiously. "The professor told me that you were at your home—have I spoilt your holiday?"

Charity reassured him. "No, not a bit of it—I decided to leave St Simon's some weeks ago and I was at home wondering what I would do next. I'm sorry this has happened, it's rotten hard luck for you, but I'm sure the professor will settle it once and for all this time. Is Mrs Boekerchek staying in Utrecht or coming over from your home each day?"

She encouraged him to talk as she started on the familiar round of pre-op preparations—indeed, by the end of the morning, she felt as though she had never been away—everyone remembered her; the radiologist greeted her like an old friend, so did Dof van Dungen and Zuster Doelsma. And the professor—he came that afternoon, looking remote; it could have been another man who had kissed her the night before. There was no expression on his face when he spoke to her, his voice was bland; she was the nurse in charge of the case, that was all.

Pride forbade her from so much as smiling at him, she answered his questions in a cool, professional voice, her green eyes as cool, schooling her thoughts in keep to the matter in hand—Mr Boekerchek. He was to go to theatre at two o'clock the following day, said the professor, and Miss Dawson would be good enough to arrange her off duty as she had done previously. She understood, did she not, went on the bland voice, that she would be expected to forfeit a good deal of her free time for the first three days?

She assured him that the arrangement suited her very well and begged him, in her best professional manner, not to give the matter a thought. He said nothing at all to this, only stared at her; it was a welcome relief when Dof asked about the pre-med, and in due course she escorted him to the door, very correct in her borrowed uniform and stiff, plain cap, where he wished her an equally correct good day.

She didn't see him again until she stood in the theatre beside the unconscious Mr Boekerchek, and when he came in he took no notice of her at all, which was, after all, only to be expected. The operation took longer than the first one had done but proved rewarding, for the professor found two more adenomata this time and that with the greatest difficulty, and after an exhaustive search for any further lurking tumours, he closed the wound with a Redivac drain and what Charity took to be a pious prayer in Dutch that this would be the last of the business.

The remainder of the day and the first part of the night allowed for no personal reflection; Mr Boeker-chek was a tough man, but the operation had been severe strain on him. He lay, once more in his space foil blanket, happily unaware of the activity going on around him, of Charity working endlessly to get him back on the road to recovery once more, of the professor standing by his bed, assessing his chances with a thoughtful expression on his handsome features. But thanks to everyone's efforts, he opened his eyes late in the evening, made a hazy remark about Charity's cap, said: "Don't cry, honey," to his wife, who was, and went to sleep again.

In the morning when Charity returned to duty again, he was still hazy but decidedly better, a fact which the professor had no hesitation in telling him later in the morning, and which he repeated when he paid an afternoon visit to his patient, and Mr Boek-erchek, much more himself now, nodded his tired head. "You look like a guy who wouldn't lie all that easily," he muttered. "I'll believe you. Where's that nurse of mine?"

"On the other side of the bed," the professor ad-vised him, "but don't try and turn round to look at her, you might fall foul of your drainage tube. We'll have it out tomorrow." He glanced across the bed. "Come round here, Sister Dawson, and let Mr Boekerchek see you; I believe he considers you a goodluck mascot."

She did as she was told without looking at him, to turn a calmly smiling face upon her patient. "That's better," said Mr Boekerchek. "The pair of you..." he closed his eyes and went immediately to sleep.

His progress was steady after that; on the fourth day after the operation Charity was able to take a few hours off duty, and delighted to be free after several days of hasty meals and long sessions in her patient's room, she changed into a sleeveless cotton dress of a delicate apricot colour and went out into the crowded streets of Utrecht. But they held little appeal for her; it was too hot for their crowded pavements and she had no shopping to do.

She wandered off down a narrow side lane and found herself in a quiet street, brick-paved, with a canal on one side of it and a row of tall, fine houses on the other. She strolled on, examining the face of each house as she passed it. They all looked rather alike, with their solid front doors and great square windows, their size suggesting that they had been built for giants to live in.

Unlike most of the Dutch houses she had seen, these had no net curtains at their windows, only glimpses of velvet or brocade hangings. The people who owned them must be rich, Charity decided, for

their upkeep would be enormous. She had come to a
halt before a particularly impressive residence; perfection itself with its fresh paintwork and shining windows, calculating how many daily helps would be
necessary for its proper upkeep, when her attention
was diverted by a car drawing up beside her—the
professor in his Daimler. She was furious with herself
for flushing at the sight of him and her colour deep-
ened still more when he remarked as he got out:

"Ah, Miss Dawson, so you have tracked me down,
have you? Can it be that your many talents include
that of detecting?"

The gross unfairness of this remark rendered her
speechless; all she could do was stare at him, her
mouth open, so that he added infuriatingly: "Close
your mouth, my good girl, you appear half-witted."

This unkind remark acted like a douche of cold
water. "And so would you," she snapped, "if anyone
dared to speak to you like that. I never heard such
arrogance!" She choked with rage and mortification.

"Rudeness, too, surely?" he prompted helpfully.
"Accept my apologies, Miss Dawson. Dear me, I
seem to be eternally apologising to you, don't I? Either my manners have become deplorable or you are
more touchy than most girls."

He had drawn her across the narrow cobbled pavement and up the double steps to the front door, where
he paused, giving her the opportunity to say furiously:

"I am not touchy—and I'm glad that you realise that your manners are quite impossible!"

He grinned at her so disarmingly that she only just stopped herself in time from smiling back at him. Instead she composed her lovely features into what she hoped was a cool mask, and seeing that there was no escape from the firm grip he had upon her arm, entered his house.

The hall was wide and cool and full of bright colour by reason of the great vases of flowers on the side tables against the panelled walls. Its black and white marble floor faded into the dimness at the back of the hall where the staircase, oak and uncarpeted, led to a half landing, then twisted out of sight. She was given little chance to see more, however, for the professor, his hand still on her arm, walked her to a double door half way down the hall. They were on the point of entering the room beyond when a portly, middle-sized figure appeared from the archway by the stairs and advanced to meet them, and the professor paused long enough to say carelessly:

"Hullo, Potter—I've brought someone back for tea, do you suppose Mrs Potter can do something about it?"

The portly man inclined his head and contrived to take a long look at Charity at the same time, "Of course, sir—would the young lady wish to tidy herself?"

Both men turned to look at her so that it was only

by a great effort of will on her part that she refrained from putting a hand to her hair or even whipping out her compact to see if her nose shone. She said "No, thank you," with dignity and smiled at the man, who smiled back with admiration, and approval and no hint of familiarity and opened the door for her. As they went inside the professor said softly: "A conquest, dear girl, you have the estimable Potter in the hollow of your capable hand. Do you always find it so easy?"

"I don't know what you're talking about," said Charity with some asperity, and fell silent as the beauty of the room struck her.

It was large and high-ceilinged with its wide windows draped elaborately with a rich cherry-coloured brocade, the same colour was under her feet; a carpet of a thick softness into which her sandals sank luxuriously. To her confused gaze everything in the room seemed of the richness found only in films and the pages of glossy magazines, and yet she could see that the furniture was used, even faintly shabby, a fact which only served to highlight the great portraits on the walls and the silver in the great glass-fronted cabinet against one wall. Her green eyes tried to take everything in at once and failing, came to rest upon the figure of a very small old lady sitting very straight-backed in a lavishly buttoned and fringed crinoline chair.

The old lady was dressed in black with an old-fashioned while lace collar, boned to stay up under her chin and a quantity of gold chains dangling down her front. She searched among them now and lifted a lorgnette on the end of one of them and peered through it at Charity, speaking at the same time in a gruff rather deep voice.

"Everard—how unusual to see you at this time of day, dear boy, and with such a pretty girl too—she is a great deal prettier than that fair-haired young woman with the lisp."

She transferred her bright blue eyes to Charity. "No doubt you are wondering why I speak in English, for I am not an Englishwoman, you know; but you, I imagine, must be the nurse Everard mentioned he would have to fetch from England." She nodded briskly to the professor, who stood listening to her, a smile on his face. "Introduce her, Everard."

Charity, the professor's hand still clamped to her arm, walked over to the old lady's chair and looked down at her with interest while her companion performed introductions with careless grace. So this would be his grandmother—she must be very old; Charity guessed, though clear enough in her mind even if she appeared frail, and she guessed too that the frailty hid a disposition of iron. She wondered how they got on together, the professor and his small, rather fierce grandmother, as she set about hedging the string of questions being fired at her.

The professor had offered her a chair near his

grandmother and gone to sit in a great winged armchair close by, taking little or no part in the conversation, if the questions being shot at her, and her
monosyllabic replies, could be called that. It was a
relief when Potter came in with the tea tray, which
he set down before Mevrouw van Tijlen with the
quiet remark that Mrs Potter had just that minute
taken a sponge cake from the oven and as the professor and his guest had arrived unexpectedly, she had
taken the liberty of sending it up.

He had barely closed the door behind him when
the old lady asked:

"You find it surprising that my grandson should
employ an Englishman?"

Charity smiled. "No, I don't think so, though I
daresay it's unusual. Probably there is a good reason
for doing so."

She was given an approving stare. "A sensible
enough answer, but you seem a sensible young
woman—nice voice, too." She poured tea and handed
the cups and saucers to the professor, who gave Charity hers without comment and went to sit in his chair
again.

"Do you like this house?" demanded the indefat-
igable Mevrouw van Tijlen.

"The hall and this room are very lovely," said
Charity politely, "I haven't seen anywhere else."

"You like antiques?" the blue eyes snapped at her.
"Portraits, jewellery?"

Charity put down her cup. "Very much, though I know very little about such things."

Her hostess snorted delicately. "Better than pretending to a knowledge you don't possess, anyway." She cast a malicious glance at the professor, who munched cake and took no notice. "Some of these modern chits... There are several interesting pieces in this house—they're Everard's now, of course." She gave him another look, but this time of deep affection. "You're not talking, dear boy."

Her grandson eyed her with a kindly twinkle. "Dear Grandmother, what chance have I had?"

"Impertinent fellow!" She allowed him to help her to a lavish slice of cake and turned her attention to Charity once more.

"My dear," she said in a voice suddenly faintly pathetic, "I'm a tiresome old woman, am I not? Everard is very good to bear with me."

"Take no notice of her," counselled her grandson cheerfully. "She's angling for sympathy, and if the truth's known, most of the time it is she who bears with me. If you've finished your tea, come and look at the silver in this cabinet—some of it is English. An ancestress of mine married an Englishman who took refuge here during the reign of Cromwell; their daughter married a Dutchman in her turn and brought the silver with her as a dowry."

Charity, very conscious of him standing beside her, examined the pieces he pointed out, made a few intelligent remarks about them and then, her interest suddenly caught, exclaimed: "What is in that little red velvet box?"

When he spoke she could hear hesitancy and surprise in his voice, and his answer was brief. "A gemel ring," was all he said, and when she waited to hear more and realised that he wasn't going to enlarge upon his meagre statement, she felt regret; she would have liked to have examined the ring—held it in her hand. Even at that distance, she could see that it was very old, the two rings skilfully locked in a design of clasped hands over a heart.

She said out loud, speaking her thoughts: "Oh, I remember—'but I return a ring of Jimmals to imply thy love had one knot, mine a triple tye'."

He gave her a sidelong glance and she couldn't understand his expression at all.

"You know your Herrick." There was faint amusement in his voice and she felt a wave of annoyance at herself; here was another item he could chalk up against her for being a know-all.

"I—I just happened to remember it," she answered lamely, and waited for him to tell her about the ring, but he made no further remark; it would be some family treasure with a sentimental tale attached to it, a tale which he would consider no concern of hers. Nor was it.

She stood awkwardly, looking away from him, until the old lady said tartly: "You won't get him to talk about the gemel ring, Charity Dawson, so come over here and talk to me.''

Charity joined her hostess once more, relieved and at the same time sorry to move away from Everard van Tijlen's disturbing presence, and amused at the little old lady's gruff commanding manner and endless questions. After ten minutes or so she made her excuses and took her leave, and the professor, who had gone back to his chair again, made no effort to detain her, but got to his feet too, saying: ''I'll see you out—I daresay Potter is having his tea.''

But whether he had been having his tea or not, Potter appeared as they crossed the hall, and went to open the door with another look of approval and a faintly complacent smile for Charity before he again took himself off in a discreet manner which was quite wasted; the professor's cool goodbye could have been uttered before an audience of thousands without causing even the faintest lift of a brow.

Charity didn't see the professor for the next two days—at least, when he visited Mr Boekerchek she was naturally there to answer his questions, but his manner was so impersonal as to be offhand, and her own manner, in consequence, became more and more wooden. It was on the third morning that Mr Boekerchek surprised everyone by having a coronary. It took their combined efforts—the professor, hastily informed, the anaesthetist, Dof and Charity—to bring him round, and even then his condition gave rise for some concern. Charity, her mind and hands full with the complex equipment needed to keep her patient alive, listened to the professor's instructions and hardly noticed when he went. The other two men followed him with the warning that they would be in theatre if they were wanted, adding the corollary that she knew what she had to do, anyhow; there was an emergency buzzer if she needed it and the panic trolley was at hand with everything on it she would need should Mr Boekerchek take a turn for the worse. She nodded quite cheerfully as they left her, knowing herself capable of dealing with whatever emergency arose, and set about the business of keeping her patient's vital organs working until such time as he should become capable of doing it for himself.

It was quite an hour later when the hospital alarm began to shrill. Charity took very little notice of it at first, she had heard similar alarms before, hospitals held fire drills as a routine, she supposed that this was one. She went on with what she was doing and was quite astonished when Zuster Doelsma put her head round the door with an urgent: "There is a fire in the X-ray department. It is quick and also severe. Patients are to be evacuated to the old wing, only those who are too ill to be moved must stay." Her glance fell upon Mr Boekerchek's far from healthy face. "He is not good, perhaps?"

"He'll do," said Charity, "but not yet. I'll stay."

She was trying to remember where the X-ray department was exactly. They had gone down two flights and through several passages—it must be miles away. "It's a good way from here, isn't it?" she asked.

"Two floors down—not near the wards, but the theatre is above it." The Dutch girl prepared to go. "I must return to the ward, you understand? You are not afraid to be alone—perhaps not for long."

"Not at the moment," said Charity, her attention more than half taken up by Mr Boekerchek's precarious condition. She looked up and grinned, "I dare say I shall be petrified when I have time to think about it, but by then the fire will be out."

Zuster Doelsma looked doubtful, but an urgent voice calling her by name gave her the time to do no more than nod before she sped away.

Charity went back to various jobs; Mr Boekerchek was improving, the pattern on the cardiograph gave proof of that, but he certainly wasn't fit to be moved. Spurred on by his colour, which was almost human again, she became absorbed in her efforts to keep it so, so that the noise of the fire engines and the far-off sounds of those engaged in putting out the fire went unnoticed. Only after a little while, when she was charting her latest findings, she remembered what Zuster Doelsma had said about X-Ray being directly under part of the theatre unit. She cast her mind back in a desperate effort to remember what Dof had said—something about a lengthy op which would take all of three hours. Her eyes flew to the clock; there was still half an hour of that period to go and the professor would be in theatre... With an effort she dragged her mind back to what she was doing—her duty lay with her patient, even though her heart rebelled.

Half an hour dragged by and Mr Boekerchek, who had been giving her a bad time of it again, was pulling round nicely when she smelled smoke. She rang the ward bell, but no one answered it, so possibly it was out of action. A nurse had been in some time earlier to tell her that all the patients had gone and was she all right on her own, and she had sent the girl away, saying that if she needed help she would ring. Now she sniffed the air again, a little puzzled. The fire would surely be under control by now and there could be no further danger. The smoky smell was decidedly stronger, but there was no question of moving Mr Boekerchek—or was there?

Charity stood quietly, trying to stay calm and assess the disadvantages and advantages of disconnecting him from all the vital instruments surrounding him and pushing his bed to the lift, or leaving him to maintain his steady improvement with the vague chance that they would both be burnt to a crisp.

She found herself laughing at the very idea and then choked on the laugh at the professor's snarling: "What the devil have you got to laugh about, Charity?"

He had come in silently, still in all his theatre gear. He had even kept his theatre boots on, and he appeared to be in a very bad temper indeed. She decided not to answer him but asked instead: "Is the fire out, sir?"

"No." He was by the bed checking his patient's condition. "The theatre is like an oven—I've left Dof to stitch up, there's no danger from X-ray now." He shot her a furious glance. "Why are you still here? Why did you not evacuate? Zuster Doelsma should have warned you."

"She did. I thought it better to stay and hope that the fire would be put out quickly. Mr Boekerchek hasn't been too well," she indicated the cardiogram with its telltale lines, "but he's improving quite well now. I was just wondering if I should disconnect him and push the bed to the further lift."

A wave of warm, smoky air wafted gently in through the door, somewhere, not close, and there was a sound like the wind blowing. The professor pushed past her and disappeared into the corridor to return very quickly. "That's your precious lift," he told her irritably, as though it were all her fault, "going up like a torch. There must have been a short circuit in the electricity. Go down to the next floor by the end staircase."

"And leave you here? I won't," she told him roundly. "If we disconnect him now and push the bed through the ward to the head of the stairs..."

The professor's eyes narrowed to grey, gleaming slits. "Don't be such a damned little fool. You'll do as I say and you'll do it now, and when you have you will find three men and send them up here to me."

It was impossible to disobey a voice like that—cold steel, and full of some feeling which she put down to bad temper coupled with a strong dislike of herself. The idea of leaving him there appalled her—supposing something frightful happened and she were never to see him again? He would never know now that she loved him with all her heart; he was never going to know anyway, she reminded herself as she sped through the ward and down the stairs, not trusting herself to so much as look at him. It was pure good luck that Dof and the houseman, with the anaesthetist close behind, were coming towards her. They were half way up the stairs before she had finished telling them that the professor and Mr Boekerchek were still in the private wing.

There was a wisp of smoke eddying around the theatre floor, but it looked safe enough and theatre Sister was providentially coming towards her.

"An intensive care room," demanded Charity urgently, "Mr Boekerchek—they're bringing him down."

The other girl nodded and darted down a short passage leading away from the theatre unit. "Here—it is the gynae theatre recovery room—it has everything necessary and the fire is not close."

They were whipping the bedclothes neatly aside as she spoke, switching on lights and heat and plugging in the sucker and oxygen and the cardiograph. They were ready when Mr Boekerchek, borne with all the care which might be accorded to the Crown Jewels, was seen in the distance.

"Here!" called Charity urgently, and received her patient with careful efficiency, to tuck him up once more and connect him to the variety of apparatus awaiting him.

The professor stood quietly by while she did this; only when she had finished did he address himself to her. "You should be perfectly safe here. I believe that the fire is now under control, and, in any case it is on the floor below and on the other side of the main corridor." Without taking his eyes off her he said to Dof: "Go and see what is happening, there's a good chap. And you," nodding to the houseman, "see what's happening in the theatre, please."

He remained silent until these two gentlemen had left to do what he asked, and although he didn't so much as glance at the anaesthetist, Charity wasn't surprised to see him going through the doors either. Which left herself and the professor, and of course Mr Boekerchek, whom one could hardly count and who wouldn't be aware of the telling-off she felt sure she was about to receive.

"And now tell me why you were laughing," demanded the professor.

She had steeled herself to face his wrath although she wasn't at all sure why he should have been so very angry with her; she still thought that she had done the right thing in remaining with her patient, and she had several arguments ready proving this. His question took her off guard; it was only when his voice sliced through these ruminations with a peremptory "Well?" that she pulled herself together sufficiently to explain about being burned to a crisp; it sounded very silly, but he heard her out, his face quiet, and then astonished her by saying: "You did quite right not to panic—you probably saved his life."

Charity stared at him. "But you were furious—you told me I should have evacuated…you shouted…"

"My feelings were strong at the time," he told her, his voice surprisingly mild. "I spoke in an unguarded moment."

She did one or two observations and charted them while she pondered this remark. What had he to be guarded about, unless it was against showing his dislike of her? She pursued the thought no further; her patient had opened his eyes.

"Mr Boekerchek is back with us, sir," she said quietly.

The American was looking intently at her. "Say, what's the almighty row?" he wanted to know in a thin thread of a voice. There was certainly a row going on, although distant; purposeful feet tramping to and fro, orders being given, and a great deal of banging and thumping.

"Where's my room?" asked Mr Boekerchek testily.

The professor went over to the bed and speaking in a calm, matter-of-fact voice, gave his patient a watered-down version of the morning's happenings. "We'll move you back very shortly," he added. "In the meantime you can be comfortable here."

Mr Boekerchek nodded weakly. "As long as you and Charity say it's OK," he stated in a whisper, and dropped off into a refreshing nap.

The professor moved to the door and Charity saw from his glance that he wished to speak to her. "He'll do," said Professor van Tijlen. "We will get him on his feet as soon as we can have him out of here—a quiet stay in the country—the sooner the better."

His eyes were on her as he spoke and they looked cold. She annoyed him, she thought unhappily, just by being there she annoyed him; no wonder he was so anxious to get his patient away. She wasn't a conceited girl, but most people liked her, and here was one—the only one who mattered—who didn't.

She agreed with him in a quiet voice and turned away from his hard stare to check the cardiogram. He had gone before she had finished.

It was remarkable how quickly the hospital settled back into its well-ordered discipline. Naturally enough, there was a good deal of excitement among the staff and a spate of exaggerated accounts given by the patients to their visitors. Mrs Boekerchek, who had heroically refrained from saying anything at all to her husband when she arrived an hour or so later, besieged Charity with questions as she walked with her to the lift, leaving Dof writing up notes by the patient's bedside.

"The professor telephoned me," she explained. "How thoughtful he is, honey—he explained about Arthur being poorly and that I wasn't to come because it wouldn't help." She stopped to sniff away a few tears. "Then he telephoned again to tell me that there'd been a fire but that Arthur was OK and getting better." She looked up at Charity's kind face. "He will get better, won't he, Charity?"

"Of course, Mrs Boekerchek, the operation was entirely successful—the professor is satisfied, and he's the one to know."

"He's coming to see me as soon as he has the time—to explain it all. I guess I'm silly not to understand all that's being done for Arthur."

"No, you're not," said Charity warmly. "You just go on coming to see him in your pretty clothes and with your hair just so—that's what he needs now."

Mrs Boekerchek stretched up to kiss her. "What a dear girl you are," she declared, and added: "You and the professor, you're a darling pair."

If only we were, Charity wished as she bade her companion goodbye. It was a pity that Mrs Boekerchek couldn't listen in to some of the professor's conversations with herself—on the other hand, perhaps it was a good thing.

It was two days later after he had examined Mr Boekerchek and pronounced him vastly improved that he paused on his way out and spoke to Charity, making no attempt to lower his voice. "Miss Dawson, my grandmother has asked me to persuade you to take tea with her again. She is sometimes a little lonely and I should be grateful if you could spare the time to do so."

He nodded briefly and strode off before she had time to frame a reply. It was Mr Boekerchek who said: "Well, now, isn't that just dandy? You go this very afternoon, honey—I've got that fellow coming from the Embassy, and you're free anyway, aren't you?"

It seemed she had no choice in the matter, the professor with his high-handed requests and not waiting for an answer, and now Mr Boekerchek behaving as though it was the greatest treat for her. She would go that very afternoon, she decided, but only because she wanted to see the old lady again, not because the professor had asked her to.

Mevrouw van Tijlen was glad to see her, and so, in his discreet way, was Potter. During the course of the afternoon, the old lady told Charity a little about him. "Over here during the last war," she explained, "got wounded and took shelter, married the girl who looked after him."

"Mrs Potter is a Dutchwoman?"

"Yes, they've been with Everard ten years now—dote on him, too. Do you dote on him, girl?"

Charity choked over her tea. "Mevrouw van Tijlen, I don't know the professor, only as someone working for him. He's a splendid surgeon."

"Humph! And that's no answer, but I'm a nosey old woman, aren't I?" She fixed Charity with a blue, beady look. "Have you wondered about the gemel ring?"

Charity put her cup and saucer down carefully, they were paper-thin porcelain and probably extremely old. "Yes," she said with admirable calm. "It has—it's unusual."

Her hostess nodded. "Give me a slice of that cake, child... The ring is old—the van Tijlen men give it by tradition to the girl they intend to marry. It has been in that cabinet for years now, and when I ask Everard when he will make use of it, he laughs and says he will not take it from there until he finds the girl he will marry. And a good thing, I must say," said the old lady fiercely, "for I would not wish him to offer it to any of the chits he has brought here from time to time." She snorted indignantly. "He is forty, almost forty-one, and when I tell him to get married he says he has too much work to do and laughs."

To Charity's consternation, her old face crumpled

and two tears trickled down her cheeks. "He says that he is too old for any young girl to wish to marry; they enjoy going out with him and spending his money, but to settle down—that is quite another matter." She sniffed and added defiantly: "He is no monk, Charity Dawson!"

"Well, I should hardly expect him to be," said Charity reasonably, "as long as he marries the right girl in the end." And that one won't be me, she told herself silently. She got up from her chair and went to sit by Mevrouw van Tijlen. "Don't worry about it," she begged her. "He'll meet the right girl one day and once he's discovered that he loves her, he'll marry her and—and love her for the rest of his life."

She spoke cheerfully, although the thought of Everard loving someone else for the rest of his life made her feel utterly forlorn. The old lady chuckled: "Just like a fairy story."

Charity nodded and agreed, her voice very cheerful, only her face was wistful.

Save for his daily visit, she didn't see the professor at all, and one week later Mr Boekerchek left the hospital, and she, naturally enough, went with him. Everyone came to say goodbye to her, excepting for the professor, who for some unaccountable reason didn't come near her.

CHAPTER SIX

MR BOEKERCHEK had been given the use of a house in the Hoge Veluwe north of Apeldoorn, about a mile from the small village of Gortel. It was forty-odd miles away from Utrecht, in delightful wooded country and wild heathland, with few main roads and, save for Apeldoorn, no large towns. The house was a middle-sized villa with a steep roof from which small windows peeped, a great many narrow iron balconies and a beautiful garden. It had been built between the wars, and although its architect had been carried away on a wave of unnecessary embellishment, it had a surprisingly charming interior.

The rooms led from one to the other, nicely proportioned and many-windowed. The kitchen was enormous, but as its present owner had equipped it with every modern gadget on the market, its size presented no problem, and at the back of the house was a garden room where Mrs Boekerchek declared that she would spend her days arranging the flowers growing in such profusion in the garden. And as for Mr Boekerchek, he was so glad to be still alive and well on the road to recovery once again that he meekly agreed to the rules and regulations his own doctor imposed upon him and made no murmur at all when Charity saw that they were carried out; probably, in a week or two, when he was feeling quite well again, he would want his own way, which, his wife had confided, he had always had but now he led the gentle life he had been ordered and as Charity told him, butter wouldn't melt in his mouth.

She didn't much like the doctor who had taken over from Dr Donker while he was on holiday; a thin stooping man with a reedy voice who had a habit of tut-tutting after every remark anyone might make. He sucked in his breath at Mr Boekerchek's scars, shook his head over the meticulous notes sent by the professor, and eyed Charity with the dim suspicion that a girl as pretty as she was was bound to be a poor nurse. As the quiet days passed, she began to long for the professor, not just for herself, but for Mr Boekerchek, so that he might breathe some self-confidence into him; she was doing her best, but it seemed to her that as fast as she encouraged him in some small activity well within his powers, along came Dr Segal to tut-tut his objections. Mr Boekerchek had been very ill, but there was no reason why he should remain so for the rest of his life.

She would have liked to confide in someone, but who? Mrs Boekerchek was happy; her husband was better and she supposed that his convalescence would be a protracted one, for like a great number of people, she had a dread of anything to do with illness and

was only too glad to leave the horrid details to someone else. She had been a little surprised when Dr Segal had vetoed any suggestion of her husband taking
short drives in a car—even pottering in the garden
with her, but as she confided to Charity, doctors always knew best.

So Mr Boekerchek spent a good deal of his day
sitting in a comfortable chair in the garden, while his
wife and Charity weeded and hoed and cut the flowers, Charity would have liked to work in the kitchen
garden too, but the dour old man who came three
times a week to trim the hedges and tend the vegetables disapproved of that, even though kindly Mrs
Boekerchek had tried to persuade him in her indif-
ferent Dutch.

Charity, therefore, when she wasn't keeping an ea-
gle eye upon her patient, contented herself with gardening and short walks in the woods around the
house. Summer was almost over, but the glorious
weather still held, after the first few days she had got
into the habit of attending to Mr Boekerchek's early
morning wants and then, while he drank his tea,
scanned the papers and read his post, going for a walk
before going to the kitchen to see to his breakfast.
This particular morning she had strolled a little further
than usual; there was a hint of chill in the air and it
had rained during the night; very soon it would be
autumn, and very soon she would be going back to
England. Another week or so and Mr Boekerchek

would go back to den Haag, not to work immediately, of course, but to get back slowly into the swing of normal life.

She toyed with the idea of staying on in Holland for a few days after she had given up the case, telling herself it was a splendid opportunity to see something of the country, and knowing in her heart that if she did so it would be in the ridiculous hope that she might see Everard van Tijlen again. "Stupid fool," she admonished herself, and hurried back to the villa.

She went in through the back garden and so failed to see the Lamborghini parked at the front of the house, so that her surprise was complete when she came face to face with the professor in the long narrow hall.

It was like being a little girl again, wishing for something and getting it with glorious unexpectedness, but she took care to disguise her delight—so effectively that her "Good morning, sir," was, to say the least, austere.

"Hullo," said the professor carelessly. "You don't look pleased to see me, but I can't expect that, can I?"

Charity had no answer, wondering why he made such a point of reminding her that she disliked him, instead she asked: "Oh—is there something wrong?"

He stood in front of her, his hands in his pockets. "No—are you anticipating disaster, or is my appearance the recognised signal for you to expect the worst?''

She stared miserably at him; seeing him again was wonderful, but it was also disastrous, for he appeared to be impatient with her, as well as not liking her. She edged away from him. ''I'll let Mrs Boekerchek know that you're here—I don't think she was expecting you. We—we haven't had breakfast yet, perhaps you would care to join her?''

He nodded. ''I'm early, I know—it is the only time I can spare. I'll take a look at Mr Boekerchek later. Keep him in bed, will you?''

It was an excuse for her not to go to breakfast, though there was nothing special for her to do before the professor trod up the stairs to Mr Boekerchek's room. The men shook hands and the professor observed: ''You look fit. I've no business to be here, really—your own doctor has charge of you, but I wanted to satisfy myself that you were almost ready to get back into harness again.'' He sat down on the bed. ''Getting out each day?'' he asked. ''Going for walks, taking little drives?''

Mr Boekerchek said a little testily that no, he wasn't. ''Charity suggested that she should drive me around a bit, and that I might potter around in the garden, but Segal won't hear of it.'' He cast a worried look at his visitor. ''Say, I'm better, aren't I? I'm not having the wool pulled over my eyes?''

The professor grinned. ''Not by me. As far as I can

tell you are practically a hundred per cent fit. Thousands of men have coronaries and recover to lead a normal life again—there's no reason why you shouldn't be one of them.'' He got to his feet. "Shall I have a look at you?"

He went over the American carefully, completely absorbed. "Nothing wrong at all," he said at length. "Let's see you up and walking."

Charity draped her patient's dressing gown around him and watched him walk around the room and then, obedient to a nod from the professor, took Mr Boekerchek's pulse. There was nothing wrong with it; he was as good as he ever would be. The professor said so with an assurance which held no doubt, then stayed to talk for a few minutes before bidding Mr Boekerchek goodbye. As he went to the door, he said over his shoulder: "I would be obliged if you would spare me a few minutes, Sister."

She would spare him the rest of her life if he wanted it, only he didn't. She followed him out on to the landing and closed the door.

"Do you want me to speak to Dr Segal?" he wanted to know. His tone was impersonal; a surgeon talking to a nurse.

"Yes, please. Mr Boekerchek is getting a little fed up with inaction, and very impatient. If I could drive him round the country, or if he might walk in the woods…"

He nodded. "I'll see about it." He looked at his

watch. "I'll go on to den Haag now. When is Segal due for a visit?"

"Tomorrow."

He nodded again and they went downstairs. "Mrs Boekerchek is in the sitting-room," Charity suggested, and turned to go upstairs again.

"You will be going back to England shortly?" he asked her, his hand on the door.

"Yes—I don't know exactly, but very soon, I should imagine."

"Back to Budleigh Salterton?"

"Yes—for the time being at least."

He grunted something and went into the sitting-room without saying goodbye, and she went back up the stairs and bustled Mr Boekerchek out of his bed and into his clothes, and pretended to herself that she hadn't heard the whispered roar of the Lamborghini as it sped away from the villa.

"And that's the last of him," she told herself fiercely, longing to have a good cry. But one didn't cry over spilt milk.

Dr Segal came the next morning and after fussing around his patient, declared rather pompously that after consultation with Professor van Tijlen, he considered that Mr Boekerchek could increase his activities considerably. Car drives, he suggested, just as though no one had suggested them already, walks in the woods, more visitors. He even, when pressed to do so, gave a date when he felt that his patient might safely return to his own home in den Haag: Ten days, he pronounced, provided that Mr Boekerchek would promise not to return to his office immediately, and then only for an hour or so each day to begin with.

He was barely out of the house before Mrs Boekerchek and Charity had their heads together, planning a picnic tea, while the invalid occupied himself happily in telephoning den Haag to ask that his car should be brought over then and there.

It was a Cadillac, far too large for Charity's taste, and the chauffeur who drove it over was patently worried that she would be unable to handle it. But a short drive round the surrounding country roads put his mind at rest; he could find no fault with her driving. She dropped him off at the nearest railway station and went back to the villa, and after a light-hearted lunch with Mr and Mrs Boekerchek, drove them deep into the Veluwe, responding with patience to her patient's well-meaning advice about her driving while carrying on a lively conversation with his wife concerning her autumn outfits.

The weather still held; she drove the Cadillac each day to some local beauty spot, and as well as that, she encouraged Mr Boekerchek to walk and work in the garden, for he was recovering fast now and taking an interest in everything now. They were within two days of their departure for den Haag when he wanted to know if Charity had any plans.

"No," she told him quietly. "I don't know when

you would like me to leave—I can go home from here…''

He cut her short in horror. "But you've had no free days," he reminded her. "You must come back with us, of course, and have a little holiday before you go back to England." He thought for a few moments. "If you stay in my employ for—say, four days after we get back home, you can use our apartment as a base and spend your days as you like—on your salary, of course. How's that for an idea, honey?''

Charity agreed readily; it would be nice to have a day or two to herself, much as she liked the Boek-ercheks, and when she was offered a small car so that she could get around and explore for herself, she was delighted. There was a lot she wished to see—Utrecht, for example. She reminded herself that she had never explored it properly, ignoring the tiny voice at the back of her head telling her excitedly that here was an unlooked-for chance to see the professor just once more.

She was aware that it was a foolish plan, but that didn't prevent her from carrying it out on the day following their return. A rather elderly Mini had been found for her, she set off directly after breakfast, un-deterred by a nasty little wind and the threat of rain from a fast clouding sky. She parked the Mini by the side of one of the canals in Utrecht and made her way to the café where she had had coffee with the Sisters from the hospital, hoping that perhaps one of them might be there, but there was no one whom she knew at the crowded tables. She realised suddenly that she was lonely, that it would have been pleasant to have had a companion. Perhaps after all she wouldn't stay until the end of her four days; she would think up some reason for going home so that the Boekercheks wouldn't be offended, and book a flight for the next day. She drank her coffee while she made her plans and went outside again; since she was here she might as well see as much as possible.

She went first to St Catherine's Convent Museums and then to the Central Museum; by that time it was one o'clock, so she had a *Kaas broodje* and some more coffee at a small café close by, sitting over it for as long as she could, for the afternoon stretched emptily before her even though she had visited only a fraction of the places in her guide book. She decided all at once to scrap them and go where her feet led her until tea time—not that she obeyed her feet, which showed a tendency to stray in the direction of the quiet street where Everard van Tijlen lived. Instead, she chose the opposite direction, away from the city centre, into a maze of quiet streets and little alleys where there was almost no traffic and few people about.

The buildings she passed were old, and used, as far as she could see, as offices and small workshops. Here and there were shops too, small, and selling only the everyday necessities of daily life, and squeezed in between these, overlooked perhaps by virtue of their very smallness, were a handful of houses, brightening their surroundings with their spotless net curtains and potted plants. It had begun to rain in earnest now and Charity had just decided to return to the heart of the city and find somewhere for an early tea and perhaps visit a few churches afterwards, when her attention was drawn to two people crossing the street ahead of her. A man and a woman, very old and dressed in rusty black, walking arm in arm, their heads bowed against the rain, their feet uncertain on the cobbles, so uncertain that the old woman faltered and fell.

There was no one in sight; Charity sprinted up the street, straightened the old man, who was on the point of toppling over too, and got down on her knees by the old woman. She had knocked herself out and already there was a red patch on one temple which told its own tale. Charity took her pulse, made as certain as possible that there were no obvious broken bones and turned to the old man. She had said she would never speak Dutch, but now seemed an occasion when the handful of words and useful phrases which she had picked up over the last few weeks might be useful. *"Huis?"* she ventured, and then: *"Waar?"*

She was understood, for the old man pointed a shaking hand across the street towards a gloomy building of moderate size. It looked dreary and institutional and was probably an old people's home. Charity picked up the old woman in her strong young arms and with the old man hanging on to her sleeve, crossed the street and mounted the steps, where she had to wait while he fumbled with the old-fashioned doorknob. The hall they at last entered was austere, and as sombre as the outside of the building, and at its far end stood Professor van Tijlen, his handsome head bent as he listened to his companion, a large woman with a massive bosom and dressed severely in grey.

He raised his head as Charity walked in, said something forceful and, from the startled shock on the stout lady's face, probably very rude, in his own language and started towards her. His companion bustled forward busily too, but he outstripped her easily and stopped in front of Charity, muttered something and took her burden from her.

"You don't need to mutter like that," said Charity clearly. "I just happened to be passing. I'm just surprised to meet you here as you are." She didn't wait for his reply but went on calmly: "She fell in the street and knocked herself out—the old gentleman is very shocked."

The professor's lip twitched. "One would imagine that he might well be," he observed mildly, and turned to speak to the stout lady, who as a consequence took the old man gently by the arm and walked him away, talking all the time in a soothing, motherly voice which was in direct variance to her appearance.

"Well, since you're here," said the professor,

"you might as well lend a hand. That door on the left, if you would be so good as to open it."

A small apartment, half consulting-room, part first aid. He laid his frail burden gently upon the examination couch, saying: "We had better have some of these things off."

Charity cast off her raincoat and began the task of getting the old lady's outer garments off, and then stood aside while the professor examined her with gentle hands. "I believe there are no bones broken," he said at length, "just a nasty bump on the head—we had better get it X-rayed. If she's clear she can be brought back here and Juffrouw Blom can look after her."

"Oh, you can't do that," said Charity earnestly, quite forgetting to whom she was speaking. "She can't come back here, it's so grey and gloomy, she would be much happier in hospital."

He took the dressing she was holding out to him. When he answered her his voice was reasonable enough but slightly impatient.

"You don't understand, how should you? It would break her heart—and her husband's—if she were moved to the hospital."

Charity was cleaning the unconscious old face conscious of surprise at the professor's concern—what did he know about broken hearts? She asked curiously: "Oh, do you know them?"

"Mijnheer and Mevrouw Bregman—they live here."

She lifted enquiring green eyes to his grey ones. "And you? Are you the consultant here?"

He smiled faintly. "I am." He went over to the desk and dialled a number, had a brief conversation put back the receiver, and said:

"And now if you will excuse me, Charity, I'll get my car." He paused on his way out. "Did you intend visiting my grandmother while you are in Utrecht? I'm sure she would be delighted to see you again."

"No," said Charity firmly, "I have to go back to den Haag—I came to—to see some museums."

"They're in the centre of the city," he pointed out blandly.

"I know that," she said a little crossly, "but I had some time to spare and I went for a walk."

His eyebrows arched slightly. "Indeed?" He swung the door open. "Goodbye to you, Charity."

His place was taken almost at once by the stout lady who was towing a thin, nondescript girl behind her. To Charity's surprise she addressed her in good English. "Bep here will take you to my sitting-room, miss. There is coffee there, you must need refreshment."

"How kind!" Charity hesitated. "But isn't there anything I can do to help?"

"No, I think not. Professor van Tijlen will be back

in a few moments to carry Mevrouw Bregman to his car and I will help him if necessary.''

She spoke firmly. Charity picked up her raincoat and followed the nonentity out of the room and down a dark passage to a remarkably cosy room, bright with gay curtains and comfortably furnished. However gloomy the place was, the stout lady had a nice little place of her own, decided Charity, and at her companion's urging, took a seat by the window. There was a garden outside, small but carefully laid out with beds of flowers, very choice flowers, she noted idly, not at all the kind of thing one would expect in an institution garden—perhaps it was a private charity of some sort with a great many wealthy patrons.

She poured herself a cup of coffee from the tray Bep had brought in and sat sipping it and wondering about the professor. It would have been nice to have seen old Mevrouw van Tijlen again, but if she went to his house he might suspect that she was anxious to see him again, too—probably he thought that already; she seemed to have the habit of meeting him unexpectedly and he had never expressed pleasure at seeing her. It was disheartening to reflect that she might just as well have had a cast in one eye or rabbit teeth for all the impression she had made on him.

These depressing reflections were interrupted by the entry of the stout lady, who sat down comfortably beside her and rather belatedly introduced herself as Juffrouw Blom. As they shook hands, she went on:

"I am the *directrice* here, but I daresay you already know that from the professor." She gave Charity a conspiratorial look. "He keeps his work here a secret, you know. You are honoured that he has told you, for only a few of his closest friends know that he runs this home out of his own pocket. He was a little surprised to see you just now—such language!" Her vast frame shuddered gently. "But that was because of the accident—I am sure that you already know that he is a man of great calm, but just now and again he—how do you say?—he erupts."

Charity was breathless to hear more; here was a side of the professor she didn't know existed. "Have you worked for the professor for a long time?" she asked.

Her companion nodded her rigidly coiffured head. "Indeed, yes. Ever since he bought this place and converted it. There are twenty small flats, as you know, and the rents the old people pay—a trifle, no more, to save their pride." She shrugged massive shoulders. "The professor's hand is always in his pocket; one knows that he is a very rich man; that he commands large sums for his work, but it is not only money, it is his time and his care of us all—" She broke off. "But of course you will know all about that."

Charity hid bewilderment and said yes, of course she understood, and how proud Juffrouw Blom must be of being in charge of such an establishment.

"Oh, I am," she was assured, "for although Professor van Tijlen prefers to remain unknown, this place is highly thought of by many people—we receive many visitors."

Charity said impulsively: "Oh, could you spare a few minutes to show me a little of it?" and added, "I have heard so much about it." Which in a way was true, for had not Juffrouw Blom talked of nothing else for the last ten minutes?

The brief glimpse she was allowed of several of the flats filled her with amazement. Gone was the gloom of the rather ugly building; each small home was gaily painted, light and airy, and filled with the occupiers' own particular treasures. "There is a waiting list," she was told, "but once they come they do not have to leave again—if one is left, then he or she stays on. They are secure, and security is important to the old."

Charity left soon afterwards, but not before she had asked where Juffrouw Blom had learned her excellent English, and been told that she had trained as a nurse in England some years after Holland had been liberated. "I am not young any more, nor so handsome, eh?" she chuckled richly, "but I am happy here; I keep the professor's secret as he would wish and I work for him until I can no longer do so, and then I shall have one of these little flats for my own. I am content, you know." She chuckled again, wished

Charity goodbye and stood on the steps to wave to her when she reached the corner of the street.

Charity was thoughtful as she walked back; she had discovered a great deal about the professor, but she had been mean about it, letting Juffrouw Blom suppose that she and Everard van Tijlen were on such good terms that she was in the secret too. She remembered what the *directrice* had said about keeping that same secret; perhaps if he discovered that she had told it, however innocently, he might give her the sack. Charity stopped in the middle of a small arched bridge spanning the dark waters of a narrow canal and stared down into it. That would never do; Juffrouw Blom, despite her formidable appearance, was a dear, it would break her loyal heart to be dismissed from a job she undoubtedly loved—besides, there would be no pleasant little flat when she retired—and had she not said herself that the professor could, on occasion, erupt?

Charity walked on, her mind made up, she would have to go and see the professor and explain so that no hint of blame could be attached to the *directrice*. Not today, though, it was already too late; she would telephone and make an appointment the moment she got back to den Haag; his secretary could book her just like anyone else, he might not even know that she was coming. All the better.

She telephoned the next morning early and was

given an appointment for four o'clock at the professor's consulting-rooms.

"I thought—the hospital—" began Charity, who hadn't given a thought to consulting-rooms; five minutes squeezed in between two outpatients would have done very nicely.

"The professor works until one o'clock in the hospital," his secretary told her, "and then he sees his private patients—you will be the last. There is nothing else possible, unless you could wait until next-week."

And write a letter from England? That wouldn't do at all. Charity settled for four o'clock and asked where she should go.

The address was in a street close to the Dom tower. She parked the Mini, squeezing in between two cars alongside the canal which dissected it and crossed the brick road to the row of sober houses facing it. Number three, the secretary had said, and sure enough, there was the brass plate with the professor's name with an impressive "ring once" engraved after it in Dutch.

Charity rang once and went inside into a quiet hall and through another door with his name on it and *Receptie* above it. The waiting room was as quiet as the hall, discreetly furnished in shades of grey with white walls and subtle touches of pale colour. Very soothing, and Charity, who by this time needed soothing, advanced across the thick carpet glad to see that there were no other patients so she wouldn't have to wait. The nurse at the desk in the corner had looked up as she went in; now she smiled and asked: "Miss Dawson. Professor van Tijlen will be a moment only, if you will sit."

Charity sat, outwardly composed in her neat cream shirtwaister, but behind her calm front her brain was seething with half-formed sentences, dignified apologies and logical reasons for what she had done. She had them in a fine muddle when the buzzer sounded gently and the nurse ushered her in through the door beyond her desk.

Everard van Tijlen wasn't sitting at his desk but standing before the window, staring out. He turned round as she went in, wished her good afternoon in the politest of voices and added: "You have parked your car very neatly—you are not afraid of driving into one of our canals?"

"Oh, but I am—only there's never anywhere else to put the car. I never seem able to find a car park, they're so..." Charity stopped, aware that the interview had begun quite wrongly; she hadn't come to talk about parking difficulties. She began again. "I won't take up more than five minutes of your time, but there is something I must explain—I think you may be rather angry..."

"Supposing you sit down and tell me about it?"

He sounded just as a good consultant should, kind

and impersonal and relaxed, as though nothing in the world could ever make him angry.

"Well," she started, "yesterday afternoon…" She darted a look at him, but he had turned to face her now and he was in the shadow. She took a deep breath. "I know about the old people's home, and—and you, I mean that I know that you pay for it and run it and it's a secret, only I let Juffrouw Blom think that you had told me about it, so she told me a great deal— she wouldn't have, you know, if she hadn't supposed… She took me over some of the flats too and told me what a lot of money it cost, and—and I thought that you spent your fees on cars and…"

"Pretty girls, perhaps?" he enquired silkily.

"Yes," said Charity miserably. There was a horrid little silence and she saw that he wasn't going to say anything, so she started off once more. "I didn't think—but then I wondered if you would be very angry if she told you that I knew and give her the sack— she said that sometimes you erupt." She had her eyes fixed on his shirt front and didn't see his slow smile; she was almost babbling by now. "She's so nice, I couldn't bear it if—I'm sorry I had to come here, for I know you don't—that is, I didn't want to come, only to explain."

He had gone to sit at his desk. When she had finished he said pleasantly: "I imagine my secret is safe with you, Charity. I think that there is no reason to say any more about it. Thank you for coming."

And that was all he was going to say. She got to her feet and started for the door, wanting to burst into silly tears, but mindful of her pride she swallowed them back to say politely: "Thank you for being so mag—mag…"

"Magnanimous?" he offered. "And now perhaps we might consider the whole tiresome business finished with. My grandmother has charged me to bring you back to my house for tea. We might go now, I think."

She said too quickly: "Oh, no, thank you—"

He had got to his feet and had strolled ahead of her to the door. "Please change your mind," his voice was bland. "My grandmother is an old lady; I am afraid that we are all in the habit of indulging her every whim."

She was instantly contrite. "Oh, I'm sorry, I hadn't thought—of course I'll come." She went through the door he was holding open and crossed the waiting-room with him and through the back of the house to a door opening on to a narrow alley where the Daimler Sovereign was parked. She got in at his bidding and sat silent during the short drive, not from choice, but because she could think of nothing at all to say.

The interview hadn't gone at all as she had planned; somehow the short, businesslike speech she had prepared and the swift, dignified exit which was to have followed it hadn't taken place at all; the professor had had it all his own way. She was mad to go to his house; it was only prolonging a misery she would have to endure for a long time to come. A clean break, she had decided, but this long-drawn-out business was tearing her heart to pieces.

CHAPTER SEVEN

CHARITY ALLOWED none of her true feelings to show in her face as she greeted the old lady, who beamed with pleasure at the sight of her, commanded her grandson to ring for tea; and ordered Charity to sit down beside her at once and tell her all her news.

"Well, I haven't any," declared Charity. "I've finished my case, you know, and now I have four days' holiday. I'm going home the day after tomorrow."

"A great pity," observed Mevrouw van Tijlen, gruffy. "So far away," she added a little obscurely, and was on the point of saying more when Potter came into the room with the tea things, giving Charity a smile of pleased surprise which caused her to give him a warm smile in return. She caught the professor's eye as she did so—decidedly sardonic, she perceived; what a low opinion he must have of her!

She turned a shoulder to him and plunged into an over-bright account of the villa where she had stayed with the Boekercheks, long before she had finished the professor had excused himself on the plea of work, and walked away. He didn't come back until tea was almost finished, a meal which Charity had enjoyed despite her hurt feelings. Years ago, when she had been quite small, her godmother had taken her for a treat to the Ritz for tea; she remembered too that day the paper-thin sandwiches, the little iced cakes, the delicate china—they were all here again, in the professor's sitting-room, only he wasn't there to share them with her. True, he accepted a cup of tea from his grandmother, ate a slice of cake in an absent-minded fashion and begged to be excused again, pausing only to tell her that he would drive her back to where the Mini was parked whenever she wished. And when she protested, he merely pointed out with marked patience that he had to return to his consulting-rooms.

When she got up to go half an hour later, Mevrouw van Tijlen caught at her hand and puzzled her completely by saying: "It is a great pity, you would have done very well." The old lady nodded her head slowly. "You are a girl of character, and that is what is needed."

Charity murmured; Mevrouw van Tijlen was very old, possibly she was confusing her with someone else, or even talking about something that had nothing to do with her at all. She felt genuine regret that she wouldn't see the old lady again as Potter ushered her in a fatherly way to the front door where the professor was waiting, looking bored. He barely gave her time to reply to the man's courteous goodbye before hustling her across the pavement and into the car. He wasn't in a good mood, she could see that. She kept

silent beside him as he took the car through the early
evening traffic, and when he reached his consulting-
rooms, she made haste to get out. His hand came
down over hers as she put it on the door handle.

"No—not yet. We shall not meet again; before you
go there are things which I wish to say to you."

Very aware of his hand, Charity found her surprised voice. "I really haven't time—there can't be
anything important you could possibly want to say to
me—I think I should go." That sounded rather rude,
so she added: "I'm glad I saw your grandmother
again. I—I enjoyed my tea." She wondered why he
gave a crack of laughter. "Now if you don't mind, I
think…"

"I do mind. You will be good enough to keep quiet
and listen to me."

He hadn't moved his hand; it felt firm and cool on
her own and when she tried to wriggle free, he tight-
ened his hold.

"Our mutual friend Arthur C. Boekerchek has
doubtless already thanked you for your services; I
should like to thank you too, Charity. You are a good
nurse, I expect you know that, and a hard-working
and uncomplaining one, as well. You are also a very
pretty and disturbing young woman—you know that
too, I'm sure. If I allowed you to do so, you could
disturb me profoundly, but I feel it is only fair to tell
you that I never had intended, nor do I ever intend
that to happen. You attracted me from the first mo-

ment I saw you, but other women have attracted me from time to time; I shall forget you, just as I have forgotten them, and in a short while I shall probably find myself a wife—someone suitable, someone who won't disturb me and take my mind from my work, someone who will run my home and make no demands of me.''

She made a small sound and he went on coolly. ''You find that selfish, no doubt—perhaps I am, but my work is important, more important than anything else in my life.'' He turned to look at her. ''You see, you had reason to dislike me.''

''Why are you telling me?'' she asked in a colourless little voice.

''To give you the satisfaction of knowing that you were right not to like me.''

There was nothing to say to that. She couldn't stay another minute, not like this, cool and calm and self-possessed when what she really wanted to do was scream and shout at him and indulge in a flood of tears. The thought of never seeing him again was something she couldn't bear to think of, she would have to get away quickly before she made a great fool of herself. She said: ''I'd like to go now, please,'' and he took his hand from hers and got out of the car and went round to open her door.

It was very quiet in the street, the houses showed empty windows and there was no one about; everyone would be at their evening meal, husbands and wives and children—she shivered and said brightly: "Well, goodbye, Professor, I enjoyed the case and I'm glad it's been such a success for you, I hope you'll have many more."

He brushed this pretty speech aside. "Dammit," he uttered with a kind of cold anger, "I've had no peace since the moment we met!"

Charity stared up at him, her feelings congealing into a solid lump in her chest, and was pulled close quite roughly. "There," said the professor savagely, "now perhaps I can get you out of my system," and kissed her hard.

She was shaking with rage and misery, but she managed, to steady her voice to say in a strained way: "I hope you will find some girl to be your doormat, Professor, someone who can't say bo to a goose and who will always agree with you and tell you how splendid you are and have dozens of simply horrid little doormats who have to wear glasses and won't know how to be naughty…" she paused for breath, appalled at herself. "Goodbye!" she uttered, and fled across the road to where the Mini was waiting. His quite unexpected shout of laughter followed her.

Charity was actually packing the last of her things on the morning of her departure for England when Mrs Boekerchek came into her room, looking excited and worried and vaguely pleased all at once. "Honey," she began, "honey, something's come up. Mrs Malone"—one of her bosom friends—"she's had a fall, concussion, the doctor says, and she's so poorly and dead set on not going to hospital—Arthur's just been on the telephone and Dr Segal wants to know if you would stay just for a week or so, and look after poor Kitty. They live on the other side of town, out towards Scheveningen. They've a lovely home and a dog and two of the dearest little children." She paused and looked beseechingly at Charity. "Can you see your way, honey?" she begged.

Charity at down on the bed. "Well, it's a bit of a surprise, but I suppose I can stay. Only I'll have to cancel my flight and telephone Mother, and I've no uniform."

Mrs Boekerchek gave her an impulsive kiss. "You are such a dear sweet girl, and don't you worry about a thing just let me get back to Arthur."

Everything was seen to; Charity telephoned her mother, chose some overalls from the selection Mrs Boekerchek had conjured up from some obliging shop and was driven away in an Embassy car to her new patient.

Mrs Malone was a thin woman, who, naturally plump by nature, had dieted herself into a state of stringiness. She hadn't liked her hair either; she had changed its light brown to an unlikely blonde, and now that she was ill, neither of these factors stood up well under examination. Her pale, pinched face had a worried frown and she became excitable for almost no reason at all. Charity had gone to see her the minute she arrived, and then, with the promise to be back within the shortest possible time, had gone downstairs to meet Mr Malone and the children. Mr Malone was short, middle-aged and devoted to his wife and it took Charity a few minutes to convince him that she wasn't going to die.

"She'll have to stay in bed for a week, perhaps— I expect Dr Segal has already told you that," she explained kindly, "this excited manner she has now will improve in a few days, so will the sickness, and then it will be just a question of keeping her quiet and content until she gets about again."

The children were rather silent, though they greeted her nicely enough, a silence made up for by Tinker, the dog, who was obviously delighted to see another face around the house. Charity fended off his exuberant greeting in a kindly fashion and rather rashly promised to take both the children and the dog for a walk just as soon as she had got herself and her day organised, and went back to her patient.

When Dr Segal arrived half an hour later, he told her that there had been no fracture—the X-rays which had been taken in hospital were clear; a week or so, he considered with some caution, and Mrs Malone should be feeling almost herself. "She is," he pointed out carefully, "rather an excitable person; she worries a good deal about her—er—appearance and she becomes quickly upset by small things." He looked at

Charity and away again. "The children are high-spirited—they go to school, but when they are home I think it is important that they should be kept as quiet as possible."

So she was to keep an eye on Jack and Tracey too—she foresaw a busy week or so, with not much time to herself. But she was a practical girl; within a couple of days she had her chores organised, the children coaxed into quietness while they were in the house, and the daily housekeeper enlisted for a couple of hours each afternoon, to sit with Mrs Malone while Charity took herself and Tinker for a walk before driving the car into town to collect the children from school.

Days off were out of the question, she realised that, and when Mrs Boekerchek telephoned to ask her to lunch she had to refuse. "No days off?" asked Mrs Boekerchek, a little put out, "and those two darling children around the place—you'll be in need of a rest, honey. When you leave Kitty, you're to come straight here for a couple of days. Arthur and I won't take no for an answer."

Charity accepted the invitation with pleasure, it would be something to look forward to and something to occupy her mind. She had promised herself that she wouldn't think about Everard van Tijlen, but it was proving difficult, especially as she had seen him twice within the week. The first time she had been on the beach with Tinker, and the Lamborghini had torn along the boulevard, too far away to see if he had a companion with him, but the second time she had had a better view; she had been driving the children back from school and the Lamborghini had been in front of her and a little to one side, and she saw, in one quick look, that there was someone with him—a girl, made a little vague by distance.

"The doormat already," Charity told herself bitterly, "being broken into her placid, secure and deadly dull future—good luck to them both," she muttered between her nice even little teeth. She didn't care if she never saw him again, a palpable lie—and useless, for he didn't want to see her.

Fortunately for her peace of mind, she saw nothing more of him for the rest of her stay in Scheveningen. Mrs Malone had improved rapidly after the first week, quickly impatient with poor Mr Malone, who spoiled her to excess and got no thanks for it. The children were allowed to see her each day too, but that wasn't entirely a success either, for she declared that they made her head ache almost as soon as they appeared.

Charity, prepared to give her patient the benefit of the doubt about the headache, found herself spending more and more time with the children, inventing games which didn't make too much noise and offering, shamelessly, small bribes to ensure peace and quiet about the house. Mr Malone, when he wasn't sitting by his wife's bed, was at his office, and when he left his wife's room, he tended to disappear into

his study and stay there. Charity began to feel sorry
for Jack and Tracey, and by the end of the second
week she suspected that Mrs Malone was sufficiently
recovered to take an interest in her home and family
once more; her memory had returned, she read a good
deal—too much—and her friends visited her frequently. She spent her days sitting about her room,
doing her nails and worrying about her appearance.

But there was no mention of Charity leaving, although her duties were changing imperceptibly from
nurse to nursemaid. She wanted to go back to England, now, away from everything which reminded
her of Everard van Tijlen—to escape became her one
aim, and when Dr Segal made one of his infrequent
visits, she asked him outright if her patient was well
enough for her to leave.

He assured her, a little unhappily, that she was
"But the children like you," he pointed out. "I believe that Mr and Mrs Malone hoped that you might
stay for a few weeks until she is quite strong again."

"She's quite strong now," Charity pointed out sen-
sibly, "and I'm a nurse, Dr Segal, not a governess,
and that's what the children need. I can't think why
Mr Malone doesn't find one for them—someone
young and fond of children."

The doctor brightened. "That is a good idea—you
would perhaps be prepared to remain until a governess is found?"

She shook her head. "I came to nurse Mrs Malone

because it was an emergency, and now she's well again. I was actually on my way home, if you remember, Doctor—I should like to leave as soon as possible."

So it was arranged, not without entreaties from Mr Malone for her to stay, a bout of tears from Mrs Malone and an outburst of temper from the children, only stemmed by Charity telling them that their father was going to find them a governess who would take them for walks and read to them and play with Tinker. They wished her a regretful goodbye, but it was already tinged with excitement at the idea of having a governess.

The Boekercheks were delighted to see her again and pressed her to stay for as long as she wanted and when she told Mrs Boekerchek that she had plans to leave in three days time, her kind hostess almost burst into tears, she brightened almost immediately though.

"We'll go shopping tomorrow," she stated happily, "and in the evening we'll go to the gala performance of that opera"—she was vague as to which one it was—"in Amsterdam. Arthur has some tickets, just in case you would be able to come with us—it will make a nice end to your stay in Holland."

It sounded fun; Charity resolutely put all thoughts of Everard out of her head and settled down to a nice cosy chat about clothes. By the time Mr Boekerchek returned from his hour or so at the office, they had planned a pleasant morning shopping, and dinner was

fully occupied with an animated discussion as to the
best colour for Charity to choose for the new dress
she intended to buy.

Mrs Boekerchek went to the best shops; she by-
passed the big stores which Charity felt would have
suited her pocket very well, and took her to the Plaats
where there were a number of small and stylish sa-
lons. "You'll find something here," she assured
Charity, leading the way into one of the plushiest of
them. They came out a good deal later with Charity
carefully carrying a large box in which lay her
dress—a long full-skirted and long-sleeved dream,
with a demure neckline, outlined with a ruching of
silk to tone with the muted blues and greens of the
organza. But it wasn't demure at all, declared Mrs
Boekerchek as they got into the taxi to go home; it
was splendidly eye-catching and very pretty and made
Charity look like a wood nymph, or did she mean
dryad?

Charity had no objection to being called anything
her companion chose. The dress was gorgeous; buying it had helped her aching heart and given her what
her father would have called a bit of stiffening. It had
cost a great deal of money, but she had had no chance
to spend much of her salary; she could well afford it.
She would enjoy the opera and tomorrow evening she
would fly home. Beyond that point she refused to
think.

Mr Boekerchek, when he saw her dressed and

ready, was suitably flattering, so were the other three members of the party who had joined them and when they arrived at the Municipal Theatre in the Leidesplein in Amsterdam, Charity was glad that she hadn't been cheese-paring over her gown; the toilettes around her were quite splendid and the accompanying escorts very correct in their black ties. She followed the older ladies to the *loge* Mr Boekerchek had booked for his party, determined to enjoy herself, and when she had taken her seat beside Mrs Boekerchek she had a good look around her. The theatre was large and rather grand; it was also crowded. She was peering down at the stalls when Mrs Boekerchek exclaimed: "Why, look who's over there!"

The professor—sitting in a *loge* directly opposite, staring at the curtained stage and taking very little part in the conversation of those with him. Charity borrowing her companion's opera glasses with little ceremony, focused them briefly upon the girl sitting beside him. This, then, was the doormat, pretty in an insipid way, nicely and expensively dressed, not a hair out of place—probably her manners were perfect. Charity, built on generous lines herself, found her slim to the point of thinness. She gave the glasses back and centred her attention upon the stage as the lights faded out and the curtain rose on *La Bohème*. She had visited the opera in England on several occasions and had enjoyed it, this performance should afford her similar enjoyment; the orchestra was very fine, as was the singing, though it was unfortunate that Mimi should be a strapping size twenty, exuding splendid health with every note. Charity found that she could enjoy it better if she kept her eyes shut. When the lights went up after the first act she had to explain this to Mrs Boekerchek, who was worried that she wasn't feeling well. "Giddy, or something, honey?" she breathed anxiously. "I was getting quite worried."

Charity reassured her and at the same time became aware that the professor had seen her. She looked away at once, but not before she had remarked his utter stillness; he might have been carved from stone. She peeped again after a few minutes and found him gone. She had barely grasped that fact when she heard his voice, calm and pleasant, greeting Mr and Mrs Boekerchek and replying courteously to the introductions being made. It was Mrs Boekerchek who cried cheerfully:

"Here's someone you know—you and Charity are old friends," and before Charity could so much as say good evening he had interposed:

"Indeed we are. May I make that my excuse for having a few words with her?"

The question was purely a rhetorical one; there was nothing for it but to walk through the door he was holding open. Her heart was beating fit to choke her, she had no feelings at all save that of delight at seeing him again, but she held on to her good sense and when he shut the door, she stood against it, ready to go inside again.

She wondered what he wanted to say to her and was surprised when he inquired mildly: "Why did you sit with your eyes shut—were you not well?"

He must have splendid sight. "It's difficult to think of Mimi as a dying TB if I look at her."

He let that pass. "You did not return to England," he stated the fact rather than asked a question, and then: "Oh, come away from that door, girl—never tell me you're afraid of me?"

She assured him in a tight voice that she wasn't; she could hardly tell him that it was herself she was afraid of; it would be so very easy to fall into his arms, he stood so close. She stifled the preposterous idea and edged warily into the corridor as she answered his question.

"No—just as I was on the point of leaving there was another case." She explained briefly about Mrs Malone and then, as the orchestra started to tune up for the second act: "Ought you not to go back?"

He shrugged enormous shoulders and she thought what a pity it was that men didn't wear black ties more often; he looked elegantly trendy although he had no embroidered shirt or frilled cuffs, but his suit was superbly cut and the tucked shirt and black tie were of the finest. She thoroughly approved of him.

His voice was silken. "You look nice too, Charity," and just for a moment, forgetting everything else, she grinned at him engagingly—but only for a moment. "You should go back," she said for a second time, longing for him to stay.

His voice was still silky. "What do you think of my doormat?"

Charity blushed. "Oh, I do beg your pardon for ever saying that—I never meant—she looks charming, so pretty and—and slim."

"I dislike thin women." His eyes roamed over her person and she felt deep satisfaction that she had bought the dress. Without stopping to think she asked: "Have you given her the gemel ring?"

The silence seemed to stretch on for ever. She stood like stone, wishing with all her heart that she could recall her words—her foolish tongue. He was so quiet that she thought he must be angry.

"No—that I shall give only to the woman I love."

Her eyes flew to his, trying to read their expression. "But you must give it to her—you must love her if you're going to marry her…"

She faltered at his low rueful laugh. "But how can I marry her? And it is your fault, Charity Dawson, for how can I ask her to marry me when I am faced with the certainty of fathering spectacled children who do not know how to be naughty?"

"I'm sorry, I'm so very sorry…" he cut her short again with his cold silky voice. "Too late. You have dogged my footsteps at every turn, you have set my well-ordered life awry and cast doubts upon my future—my peace of mind is destroyed.''

She was appalled and she had no answer, but presently she managed in a whisper: ''If there is anything—anything I can do to put things right, I'll do it gladly, truly I will.'' With a childish desire to please him she added: ''I'm going back to England tomorrow, really I am, so you won't have to see me again— I'm sorry I've upset your life—I haven't meant to.'' Indeed she had not, quite the reverse; the knowledge made it impossible for her to say any more, so she slid back to the *loge* door, and without saying goodbye, slipped inside.

For the rest of the opera she sat with her eyes glued to the stage. Only when the lights finally went up and Mrs Boekerchek waved cheerfully at the professor and directed her in kindly fashion to do the same did she glance fleetingly in his direction and lift a stiff hand in answer to his curt unsmiling bow.

Somehow she got through the rest of the evening; the drive back, the cheerful talk, the vague plans for her return to Holland and then the cheerful goodbyes. She had to get through a more intimate half hour with the Boekercheks too, for they insisted upon a little chat and a final drink before they went to bed. Only when she had packed the lovely dress away and got into bed did she give way to her feelings. She would look a fright in the morning, but what did that matter?

CHAPTER EIGHT

MR BOEKERCHEK, after a leisurely breakfast, had left to go to his office for a couple of hours and Mrs Boekerchek was still in bed. Charity was on her way back from her bath and a cup of coffee in the kitchen when the telephone rang and in answer to her hullo the professor said: "Charity."

Through her sudden excitement she fancied that he had spoken her name with urgency. She said carefully so that he shouldn't hear how excited she was: "Good morning, Professor," and was rewarded by a small exasperated sound.

"When are you leaving?" he wanted to know.

"My flight goes this evening. I'm leaving here this afternoon, I want to…"

She was cut brusquely short. "Don't go, Charity. I'm coming over to see you. I'll be there within the hour, there is something I have to talk to you about."

"Well…" she began, but he had already rung off. She sat down by the telephone table and tried to think clearly, a task much impeded by the chaotic state of her mind. Why should he wish to see her? He had seen her last night and the meeting had hardly been to either's advantage, had it? Indeed, she had had the

160

distinct impression that he regarded her as a nuisance in his life and would be glad to be shot of her. But he had said that he wasn't going to marry the door-mat...

Charity leaned back and allowed herself a delicious flight of fancy; supposing he had discovered that he loved her—it seemed unlikely, but just supposing—it would be a natural thing for him to rush to den Haag and tell her, wouldn't it? After all, he hadn't known until she had told him that she was going back to England today. But here common sense crept in; she was forced to admit that he hadn't known that she was in Holland either, and if he had been in love with her, he would have been in England by now, looking for her.

He had gone looking for her when he wanted her to nurse Mr Boekerchek. She sought for an excuse and found it in the natural assumption that he had been too busy. But what about a letter, or the tele-phone? She dismissed these at once. One did not pro-pose by telephone, not someone like the professor at any rate, and members of the medical profession tended not to write letters unless they were forced to—they had secretaries, and when they had a few minutes to spare they dictated their correspondence, and no man could possibly dictate a proposal of mar-riage, or even a love letter.

She was aroused from her daydreaming by Mrs Boekerchek's voice calling from her bedroom.

"There you are, honey," said that lady, still a little sleepy. "I reckon I'll have my coffee in bed. Have you had your breakfast?"

Charity drove her thoughts sternly back to more sober channels. "Yes, thank you," she answered, and remembered that she hadn't. "I'll go and tell Nel, shall I?"

But instead of doing so she sat down again on the side of the bed and stared happily at nothing.

Mrs Boekerchek, who had composed herself for another short nap, opened her eyes again. "You feel all right, honey?" she asked anxiously.

Charity smiled. "Marvellous. Professor van Tijlen telephoned just now—he wants to see me before I go, he said he'd come over right away—you don't mind?"

Mrs Boekerchek sat up; this was far better than another nap. "Well, now, isn't that nice? I did wonder why he wanted to see you last night. Do you know why he's coming?"

Charity got off the bed. "No—at least, I'm not sure." She smiled again, deliciously, still wrapped in her foolish dreams. "I'll go and see about your breakfast and then I'd better get dressed."

She drifted away to the kitchen where she cut herself a slice of bread and butter and took it back to her bedroom to eat while she decided what she should wear. The green jersey, she judged, would do nicely, and she began to dress feverishly.

She was ready, nicely made up, delicately scented and with her hair brushed into a tawny topknot, when the apartment bell rang. Mrs Boekerchek's quite unnecessary: "There he is, honey," still echoed down the hall as she opened the door.

Professor van Tijlen walked in with the briefest of nods and once inside, asked urgently: "Where can we talk?"

She opened the sitting-room door, her silly dreams evaporating under the briskness of his manner; anyone looking less like a man in love she had yet to see, but still hope died hard; he wasn't a man to show his feelings upon his handsome face; perhaps he had been anxious about her leaving before he could see her. His first words bore out her guess, and her spirits, fed by heaven knew what romantic ideas, rose.

"I was afraid that you might have caught an early flight."

She sat down composedly and waved him to a chair. "You didn't want to know last night, you could have asked then."

"There was no need at that time—it was only this morning when Corrie telephoned me that it became so vital to stop you."

"Corrie?"

He sounded impatient. "Juffrouw Blom."

His words sank like leaden weights into her brain and tore the dreams to shreds. She picked a tiny thread of cotton off the pleated skirt of the green dress; a pretty dress, she thought idly, and quite wasted on her companion. There was no point in her speaking: he was obviously intent on telling her in his own good time what it was all about—besides, there was a lump in her throat which would choke her if she so much as opened her mouth. She had been a fool to imagine even for one moment that he was even faintly interested in her—hadn't he given proof of that over and over again?

She straightened her shoulders and gave him a look of calm inquiry.

He said heavily: "Corrie fell down early this morning and sprained her ankle. She is a heavy woman, as you know, and it happened before anyone was about, there was quite an interval of time before I could be told and get her to hospital to have it X-rayed and bandaged. She is in considerable pain, but she insisted on going back to the Home, to her own bed. She will have to remain there for three or four days before she can start passive movements and I can put on a visco-paste stocking, and then another ten days before she can do without it." He paused and studied Charity's face. "You know what I have come to ask of you, don't you? You see there is no one else—no one else who knows about the home. Corrie's assistant is on her annual holiday—Spain, I believe, and although she has a splendid staff they are none of them capable of the nursing side of the job, nor have they any authority."

"You will forgive me," said Charity rather coldly, "if I'm a little surprised that you should ask me to do this after the talk we had."

"Ah, you forget," his voice was silky once more, "I remember most clearly that you said you would do anything. Your exact words were: 'Anything I can do to put things right, I will do gladly, truly I will.'"

"Yes, but that was about the doorm…about…" She didn't even know the girl's name; she couldn't go on calling her the doormat for ever.

He got to his feet; there was neither impatience nor annoyance upon his face. "I understand," he moved to the door. "Well, I must get back."

Charity reached the door at the same time as he did. "I'll come," she said in a goaded voice. "You'll have to wait while I pack some things—it won't be for long, will it? I can come back and get the rest if I need to."

He was standing very close to her. "You mean that?"

"Yes, of course. I—I owe it to you, don't I?" She looked at him with her calm green eyes and made to slip past him, to be caught and held and kissed with a kind of controlled savagery which took her breath. Not the kind of kiss, she thought incoherently, which the doormat would stand for.

He let her go at once and disconcerted her very

much by exclaiming: "Now why on earth should I have done that?"

She was saved from answering this awkward question by the entry of Mrs Boekerchek, wrapped in her dressing gown and agog for news. Charity, leaving the professor to explain, went away to stuff a few necessities into her overnight bag and tidy her slightly flurried person. She had never been kissed like that before, and it had knocked the sense out of her head. Possibly, she thought unhappily, that was why he had done it.

They spoke little on their journey to Utrecht; it was still early, but the morning traffic was thick on the road and the professor was driving the Lamborghini with a ferocious patience which warned her to hold her tongue. Only when he made some chance remark did she answer briefly, and when he drew up before the Home she got out without a word and waited while he got her case, before walking beside him through its austere door, into the dark hall and up the stairs.

Juffrouw Blom, outsize on her feet, was truly enormous in bed, a fact considerably enhanced by the voluminous garment she was wearing. It was of some white cotton material, cut high at the neck and with long full sleeves; a kind of tent, Charity decided, eyeing it fascinated. Juffrouw Blom was frankly a very large woman, but was she justified in concealing herself in such a garment? She pondered the problem while the professor greeted his patient briefly and then turned to her.

"Charity, I must leave you now—I have a list," she guessed he was already late for it. "Juffrouw Blom will explain everything which has to be done. I'll do my best to call in some time today."

He nodded briskly, said something in a gentle voice to Juffrouw Blom and went away.

Charity turned to her companion. "Oh, well," she observed cheerfully, "there's nothing like being thrown in at the deep end," and remembered as she spoke that she would have to cancel her flight and do something about getting her fare back. No one, now she came to think about it, had mentioned money— presumably she was to be paid—and there were the rest of her clothes to fetch. She would have to worry about these things later on, but now she obeyed Juffrouw Blom's injunction to draw up a chair and have everything explained to her.

It took quite a time, and when finally Charity had a clear picture of her duties, it was almost noon. Bep, the most senior of the assistants, had brought in coffee, conferred briefly with her superior, shaken hands with Charity, and departed again, presumably to do something about the midday dinner, a communal affair to save the old people too much work and to ensure that they had the right diet.

"Bread and cheese and jam," stated Juffrouw Blom, "is what they would eat if they were on their own. They pay…'' she laughed hollowly, ''what they pay covers perhaps the cost of the potatoes; the bills for the good meat and vegetables and ice-cream go to Professor van Tijlen, and when I point out to him that these things cost a great deal of money, he laughs, nicely, of course, but of economy he will not hear a word. Rich he may be,'' she went on, half grumbling, ''but it is not right—he pays me a great deal too much, as well, and when I tell him this he laughs again and pats my arm and says: 'Go and buy yourself something pretty to wear.'''

She cast her rather fine eyes up the ceiling and sighed. ''Me!'' she said, chuckling.

Charity had listened to every word, fascinated. It was marvellous to hear about the professor—the professor she hadn't known about; even though she loved him, she had thought of him as an elegant and cool man who, although he worked hard, liked the good things of life. Now she saw that she had been mistaken; that he was warm-hearted and generous and capable of inspiring loyalty and affection, and that this was a part of life which he kept secret from almost everyone. She leaned forward and said earnestly: ''You know, the professor's right—you'd look super in a blue nightie with a round neck and those little cape sleeves—I saw some in den Haag last week.''

Juffrouw Blom stared at her. ''You think so? But I am a mountain.'

"Never mind that, mountains can be the right shape, can't they? Look, when I go back for my things, will you let me get one, just to see? It might please him enormously to see that you have taken his advice."

"I had never thought of that." Juffrouw Blom's severe features relaxed into a smile. "Yes, let us do that." She looked at Charity sharply. "You will not laugh? And the professor..."

"He won't laugh," said Charity gently, "and I certainly won't. And please will you call me Charity?"

"Indeed, yes, for I feel that we are to be friends, and you must call me Corrie."

Charity rose. "I'd love to. Now I'm going to get something for that ankle—it's getting painful, isn't it?—and then I'll go and see about your lunch. Bep goes off duty this afternoon, you said, so if I change into an overall, and have lunch too, I can take over while you have a nap, can't I?"

When she got back with Corrie's lunch it was to hear that the professor had telephoned to say that he had cancelled her flight and would arrange the refund; he had also telephoned her father.

"Good lord!" exclaimed Charity, much struck by his thoughtfulness. "You know, I'd quite forgotten to do that."

"It is not necessary to worry," Juffrouw Blom assured her, "Professor van Tiljen thinks of everything."

Charity spent a busy day getting to know the occupants of the home, doing what she could for the
invalid, who was in considerable pain, and making an
early evening round to check that all the occupants
were well and not worried about anything. She had
had no experience of such work, but it seemed to her
that the old people in the professor's care were happy
and content and enjoyed small luxuries which presumably his wealth made possible. There was no lack
of equipment in the surgery; it held everything necessary to deal with an emergency, the communal dining room was an eye-opener to her too, with its small
tables, and gay curtains, its flowers on the window-
sills and colourful pictures on the walls, and beyond
it was the recreation room, cosy with easy chairs and
small tables, shelves of books, a TV in a corner and
a piano on a little platform. There were flowers here,
too, and she noticed that the chairs were old-
fashioned and high, just the kind of chair the old people would have had in their own homes. Her heart
warmed towards Everard's kindliness even while she
wondered why a highly successful surgeon with all
he could possibly want in the world should choose to
spend his wealth and his time on the old, and probably the forgotten inmates of the home. She would
have liked to have asked him. Her tour finished, she
went back to Juffrouw Blom, helped her to prepare
for the night and then sat down with pen and note-

book, ready to be told what she was to do on the following morning.

She had got no further than the first details about early morning pills and injections to be given before breakfast; as far as she could discover, it would be necessary to make a series of domestic visits at an early hour. She looked with a new respect at her companion, who, as far as she could make out, worked a sixteen-hour day and enjoyed it. Her pen was poised ready to take down the next lot of instructions when Juffrouw Blom lifted a majestic arm and said simply: "He's coming."

A moment later the half-open door was thrust wide and the professor walked in. He was, as always, impeccably dressed, still in the fine grey cloth suit he had worn that morning; his shoes had lost none of their gloss, his linen was immaculate, but over and above these things Charity could see that he was bone weary. Little lines of fatigue ran from his nose to the corners of his mouth, there was the faintest of frowns between his brows. She exclaimed impulsively: "You're tired. You should be at home, going to bed."

He gave her a long, considered look and walked over to Corrie.

"Sound advice, dear girl, but why condemn me to my lonely bed when I have two such charming ladies to visit?" He gave her a mocking smile as he spoke and addressed himself to Juffrouw Blom. "Well, Corrie, how has the day gone? Let me take a look at that ankle.''

Charity addressed his broad back. ''Would you like some coffee?''

He didn't turn round. ''Yes, please—and a sandwich if it isn't too much trouble.''

So that was why he looked so tired. ''When did you last have a meal?''

He sounded vague. ''Oh—one, two o'clock—between lists.''

Of course he had been fetching her when he should have been in theatre.

''And this evening?''

He cast her a look over his shoulder and said almost apologetically:

''Well, I had to catch up with my work somewhere.''

Charity knew her way around the kitchen by now; she was back in no time at all with a nicely laid tray and when he got up to take it from her, she told him to stay where he was and put it on the table close by. When she took the cover off the dish by the coffee pot he leaned forward to inspect the generous portion of scrambled eggs on buttery toast and smiled at her with such charm that her heart turned right over.

''My dear girl,'' he exclaimed, ''I had no idea that you could cook. You are indeed a woman of parts.''

''Eat it before it gets cold,'' she suggested matter-of-factly. ''And I can't cook, only that.''

He began to make vast inroads into his supper. "Perhaps I should marry you," he remarked to outrage her. "Think how convenient it would be when I get home from a night emergency to find you there, waiting with coffee and scrambled eggs."

His brief, mocking glance silenced her; it was Corrie who answered him. "What nonsense you talk, Professor," she told him comfortably. "You would be the last man to expect your wife to get up in the middle of the night to cook for you."

He speared a mouthful of egg. "Dear Corrie, I am the last man to expect a wife…"

Juffrouw Blom was on to a topic close to her heart. "That, if I may say so, is nonsense—here you are, a man of no more than forty, and in the ten years in which I have known you…"

"Is it really ten years?" he interrupted her smoothly. "And that reminds me—Charity, may I have your ticket? I'll see about getting a refund for you. You don't have much luck in your efforts to get home, do you?"

His manner was coolly friendly, so she answered him in the same vein, adding: "Thank you for telephoning Father—I quite forgot to do so."

"I'm not surprised. I must apologise for rushing you in the way I did, but we were in a fix, were we not, Corrie? This place falls apart when Corrie is ill you know."

He drank the last of his coffee. "You will need

some more clothes, I daresay. You will be taking over Corrie's free time, presumably? I'll take you over to den Haag tomorrow afternoon—will it take you long to pack?''

"Ten minutes or so."

His eyes widened with laughter. "Another virtue," he murmured. "Perhaps I should snap you up after all."

But Charity was prepared now; if his manner was to be one of cool, friendly banter, then hers would be the same. They would be seeing each other fairly frequently for the next week or so. He had been very outspoken with her at the opera; she knew now exactly where she stood in his opinion, and since they had to meet, she supposed that a light-hearted burying of the hatchet, however temporary, was by far the best way to deal with an awkward situation. Not that he had shown any sign of awkwardness, she thought it unlikely that he would. She felt awkward herself, though. To hide it now, she took the tray away to the kitchen and was so long tidying it away that by the time she got back, he had gone.

He came too early the next afternoon; she was still running round with *Mist Mag Tri* for the elderly stomachs that needed it, and escorting those who usually rested to their flats, to take off their shoes for them and tuck them up on their beds. She had just left Mijnheer and Mevrouw Laagemaat comfortably side by side in their crowded little bedroom, and was flying downstairs to see Bep, when she bumped into him on the landing. She had no way of stopping her headlong flight, except by tumbling into his arms. They felt hard and at the same time gentle around her as she made haste to disentangle herself.

"So sorry," she was breathless for more reasons than running downstairs. "You're early, but I won't be more than five minutes. Have you seen Corrie?"

"Not yet." He was laughing down at her. "You may have ten minutes if you wish, I'll stay with her until you're ready. Is there anything you need to report while I'm here?"

She shook her head. "Everyone seems well and happy. I thought Mijnheer Laagemaat was a little breathless when he went to lie down just now, but he said he felt all right—perhaps he was just tired."

"Probably," he agreed dryly, "he is eighty-two. You manage to make yourself understood?"

She answered without thinking. "Oh, yes—I've been in Holland long enough to have picked up some Dutch—as long as it's basic, I can manage."

She went to pass him, but he barred her way. "And yet I remember," he told her blandly, "that you were extremely annoyed with me when I pointed out that your stay here would give you an opportunity of learning our language."

She was immediately on the defensive. "Yes, well—of course I was annoyed—you only said it to annoy me; you were very unpleasant, you often are,'' she finished recklessly.

"My dear good girl, put yourself in my place. Did I not tell you that you dog me at every turn?"

"Then if you dislike me so much," she flared, "why bother to come tearing along—at my great inconvenience, mark you…" her voice rose as her feelings strengthened. "Each time I pack to go home, you come along with some—some reason why I can't go."

She was stopped by the look on his face; a look she couldn't understand at all. He said slowly: "So I do," and stood back to let her pass. She was conscious of his eyes on her back as she ran downstairs.

She speculated briefly about it as she changed, and because there was no time she brushed her hair into a ponytail, snatched up her handbag and tore along to Corrie's room. Their trip would take up most of the afternoon. The least she could do, however unpleasant he was, was to save as much time as possible. Why he should go to so much trouble to help her when he was so consistently rude to her, she couldn't imagine. And yet she loved him. Seeing him leaning against Juffrouw Blom's massive wardrobe, waiting for her with no sign of impatience, merely strengthened that feeling. She was sure now that she would always feel like that, even if, despite his disclaimer, he married his doormat.

Apparently they were to be on good terms again;

the drive to den Haag was nothing but pleasure, with her companion talking about everything and everyone under the sun save himself; even when she ventured to ask him why he had opened the old people's home, he put the question gently aside without answering it. She should have had more sense, she thought bitterly, than to ask him questions like that; she would be the last one to share his ideas on life, and yet, to her annoyance, she found herself telling him quite freely of her own life and home when he asked. Not that there was much to tell; for she really had only the vaguest idea of what she would do. A job in some hospital, naturally—but a week or two's holiday first; it was early autumn, and Budleigh Salterton could be delightful at that time of year.

Mrs Boekerchek was waiting for them, embarrassingly arch in her manner but unfailingly kind in her offers of help and when Mr Boekerchek came in, looking almost well and full of himself once more, Charity slipped away to collect the rest of her belongings. She was back again in a commendably short space of time to hear the professor refusing an offer of tea as he had urgent business to attend to before he returned to Utrecht. She concealed her surprise, bade her friends goodbye with a promise to see them again before she left Holland, pretended not to hear when Mrs Boekerchek wanted to know in a whisper if there was a romance blossoming, and accompanied the professor to his car. He stowed her case and got in beside her.

"Corrie told me that you have some vital shopping to do for her; that is why I refused the offer of tea— I should have mentioned it."

"Have you the time?" she asked quickly. "I hadn't liked to ask you because I thought you would be in a great hurry. I didn't know that Corrie had told you."

"Only that she wanted you to buy something for her. I gather I'm to be surprised later."

Charity smiled. "That's right. Corrie's such a dear, why ever didn't someone marry her?"

"He was killed in the war. I should be lost without her—she's sound right through, and so kind. She likes you."

"I like her. Could we go to one of the big stores? Metz will do."

She found what she wanted with no trouble and bore it triumphantly back to the patient professor. He eyed the package with some interest. "Have you been putting frivolous ideas in Corrie's head?" he asked.

"They were there already. I hope I haven't wasted too much of your afternoon, it was very kind of you to bring me over."

"I am not an unkind man," he assured her gravely, "and upon reflection, I haven't wasted my afternoon." He glanced at his watch. "If you have really finished, I suggest that we go straight back and have tea with Grandmother."

"Will there be time for that? I don't think I should—I told Bep I would be back…"

"Half past five—I made that clear to her, that gives you ample time to do the medicine and injection round before the old people sit down to their evening meal." His eye fell upon the package. "Should I call and see Corrie this evening?"

"Oh, would you, that would be…" She paused in thought. "I suppose you couldn't possibly tell me when, so that she's…"

"Half past eight—no, eight o'clock," he obliged readily. "I can only stay a few minutes, though; I have a dinner date." He shot her a wicked glance. "The doormat," he told her silkily.

She felt the chill of disappointment and her voice was stiff as she answered him.

He had manoeuvred the Lamborghini ahead of a succession of cars and had a free road for the moment, and he was driving with a relaxed expertise which was a joy to watch. Charity concentrated on that for a few minutes before asking: "Perhaps you would rather take me straight back to the Home—that would give you more time…"

"Do I want more time?" his voice was innocent. "Perhaps you think that I should go into a brown study and concentrate on the—er—doormat, without you to distract me." He threw her a sidelong glance, his eyes alight with amusement. "It takes a good deal to distract me, Charity."

"That is not what I meant," she said with a decided snap. "I have never met anyone like you..."

"A point in my favour. How are you enjoying the job?"

So the hatchet was to be buried again. "Very much. I had no idea that it could be so interesting—no wonder Corrie loves it. When I first saw it, the Home looked so gloomy, but inside it's simply marvellous. Is there a waiting list?"

"Yes, a long one. I'm looking out for another place to convert—a friend of mine in Amsterdam thinks he has found the very thing. I must go and see him about it. He's married to an English girl." He spoke carelessly. "Perhaps you would like to come with me and meet her." Not giving her time to answer, he went on: "You're free on Saturday, aren't you, and that is when I intend to go."

There was nothing in the world she would rather do, although it seemed strange that he should ask her when they annoyed each other so much—besides, what about the doormat? She answered carefully: "But wouldn't you rather take—take..."

"Away for the weekend." His reply was laconic.

"In that case, I should like to come very much—your friends won't mind? I shan't be in the way?"

"On the contrary," he remarked with unflattering candour, "you and Abigail can sit and worship the baby while Dominic and I are left free to talk."

So that was why he had asked her to go. Charity

sat silent until they got out of the car and when he said kindly: "My grandmother will be pleased to see you, Charity," she couldn't help wondering if he found her a dead bore and a nuisance into the bargain, but just because the old lady had taken a fancy to her, he was putting himself out to be civil. This unhappy theory was substantiated presently, for he drank a cup of tea and then left their company with the excuse that he had some telephone calls to make and would return in time to take Charity back. She had no time to brood about this, however, for the old lady was full of questions about her job and Juffrouw Blom's ankle and when did she intend to return to her home.

Charity forbore from saying that she intended to go home the moment she was given the chance to do so, but she refrained, merely explaining patiently that she would leave just as soon as Juffrouw Blom was on her legs again. "I don't have to wait until she is quite recovered," she went on, more for her own benefit than that of her listener. "As soon as she can get around a little, I shall feel free to go."

"You'll not come back?" The old lady's eyes were sharp.

Charity smiled, nicely in command of herself because the professor wasn't there. "I don't suppose so. The Boekercheks have asked me to visit them, but you know how it is—once I have gone, I shall be forgotten—that's natural."

Her hostess nodded her head. "Quite natural child,

but there are exceptions to every rule. Some people one meets remain in one's mind for the rest of one's life.'' Charity jumped visibly when she went on, "Everard will remain in yours, I fancy.''

A question which would have to be answered, judging by the lynx-eyed look she was getting from her companion. "Well, yes," said Charity, rather proud of her noncommittal voice. "You see, I've done a lot of work for him..."

"I don't mean that." The gruff old voice was impatient.

"Yes," said Charity simply.

"I thought as much."

"I should hate him to find out," said Charity humbly.

"Not from you, he won't—nor, I need hardly add, from me. Your secret is quite safe, Charity." She went on in a cross voice: "He's taking out that whey-faced van Stassen girl this evening; she's only half alive, and the live half isn't at all to my liking."

At which remark Charity couldn't help but laugh, so that when Everard, coming back to fetch her, wanted to know what was so amusing she hesitated over a suitable reply, it was Mevrouw van Tijlen who came to her rescue with some observation about the amusing people she had met as she put up her old face to be kissed by her grandson, and when Charity bent to shake her hand, she kissed her too.

There seemed to be a great deal to do when she

got back. She had handed over her shopping to Juffrouw Blom before she began on her evening's work, and it was an hour or so before she went back to that lady's room, to find her sitting up in bed, decked out in the pale blue lacy confection Charity had chosen. She walked round the bed slowly, viewing the occupant from every angle. "It's perfect," she pronounced. "You look sweet and it makes you heaps younger and much slimmer. Those little sleeves are just the thing."

"It is not too girlish?"

"Heavens, no. Why should you wear dull undies just because you're past your first youth? Don't you feel better for wearing it?"

Juffrouw Blom nodded. "It is true, even though there is no one to see, I feel both young and gay; I shall buy more of these pretty things and throw this away." She tossed the white cotton tent on to the floor and Charity was bending to pick it up when the professor knocked and came in. He looked remarkably handsome; surely the doormat was looking forward to her evening, thought Charity, wishing him a sober good evening. He accorded her a brief, casual nod; clearly his visit was for Corrie, for he went straight to the bed and after eyeing her for a moment, said: "Well, Corrie, how very nice you look—that silk thing suits you. Why ever have you been wearing those tents all these years? Was this the secret shopping?"

Corrie chuckled richly. "You have said so many times that I should buy pretty things, Professor, and now I do so—I was a little afraid until Charity persuaded me, for I thought that you might laugh."

He sat down on the edge of the bed and took one of her hands in his. "No, Corrie, why should I laugh? You look delightful, and I beg you to buy all the pretty clothes you have a mind to, for you are still far too young to wear all these dreary greys and blacks. As soon as you are on your feet we will go shopping—new uniforms, I think, blue this time, or brown, and a different style. Which reminds me, if I don't take a look at that ankle now, you'll not be on your feet for days, and we don't want that."

He left shortly afterwards, leaving Juffrouw Blom in a warm glow of content and Charity ice cold with misery, imagining the evening he was enjoying in Juffrouw van Stassen's company.

She didn't see him the next day, and the morning after that, when he came to strap Corrie's leg, he gave her little of his attention, nor did he stay for coffee, pausing only to warn her that the physio would be along to start Juffrouw Blom's exercises. "Once you're on your feet," he declared cheerfully, "we'll have you back at work in no time," he turned a blandly smiling face towards Charity, "and then Charity will be out of a job once more."

It seemed he couldn't wait for her to go; she went

through the day in a fine temper, well concealed and therefore all the harder to quench.

She was doing her evening round when he telephoned her. "I shall call for you tomorrow morning at half past nine," he informed her. "It will be Saturday, you know."

"Oh, yes—well, if you still want me...!" began Charity, caught off her stride.

"Half past nine," he repeated, and laughed gently "Goodnight."

She wore the green jersey again, because it was getting chilly now and everything else she had was too thin, and because the morning was overcast, she took her raincoat, wishing she had something more glamorous to wear. She looked a little pale when she went to say goodbye to Juffrouw Blom, already dressing-gowned and sitting in her chair, busy with laundry lists and the like, and that lady, scanning her face, offered the opinion that it was high time she had an outing of some sort, for she looked quite pasty-faced. The professor made a similar remark as he opened the car door for her to get in, although he put it down to working too hard. "And I daresay you find it a little dull after hospital life," he commented as they started on the twenty-six miles to Amsterdam.

She protested vigorously: "Indeed I don't—Corrie is such fun, and the old people are sweet. Of course, we can't talk a great deal, but it's wonderful what one

can do with a dictionary and a bit of arm-waving.''
She paused. ''Did you have a pleasant evening?''

''Yes. It's nice to get these matters settled,'' he
observed, just as though, she fumed silently, she knew
what he was talking about. When he didn't say any
more she began a conversation about the weather, in
which he joined; she could hear the laugh in his voice
and wondered why he found it amusing.

The van Wijkelens' house was large and old and
tucked away in a small cutting off one of the main
canals. Its massive front door was opened by an elderly man who addressed them in a friendly Cockney
voice which surprised Charity, especially as her companion seemed to know him very well. ''This is Bol-
linger,'' he explained. ''He came to Amsterdam with
Abigail, and has stayed ever since,'' and when she
had shaken hands: ''Where is everyone, Bolly?''

''Up in the nursery, sir, if you and the young lady
like to go up.''

They climbed the staircase side by side. There was
a good deal of laughing and talking coming from
across the landing; a door was half open and Charity
could see the van Wijkelens. He as tall as Everard
and equally good-looking and his wife, surprisingly,
small and plain; but plain in an interesting fashion,
Charity had to admit as they were discovered, wel-
comed and taken to admire the baby in his cot—a
delightful small creature, bathed and fed and about to
take his morning nap.

On the landing again, Abigail van Wijkelen led the way downstairs. "I hope you didn't mind," she said in her gentle voice, "but he's rather new, you know, and we're so very pleased with him."

This remark led, naturally enough, to an interesting conversation between the two girls concerning babies, Abigail's small son in particular, and then, by a natural sequence of events, to clothes; they were still discussing the newest fashions when the gentlemen disappeared into Dominic's study, leaving the girls to pour more coffee and settle down for a cosy chat.

"Everard doesn't come very often," volunteered Abigail, "he's so busy—but I think Dominic has found him a suitable house…" She stopped. "You do know about Everard's…oh, dear, have I dropped a clanger?"

Charity laughed. "No, it's all right, I know all about it. I discovered it quite by accident. I'm working there now, as a matter of fact, because Juffrouw Blom, who runs the place for him, has sprained her ankle."

Which remark called for more explanations. They were still deeply engrossed when the men came back and Abigail said at once: "Dominic, isn't it a shame that Charity has to go back to England in a few days? There are so many of us she could have met." She turned to Charity. "There's Sophy Oosterwelde near Utrecht, too, she's married to another friend of Everard, and they have a boy and a girl—it would have been so nice…''

"Yes, wouldn't it?" Charity agreed hastily, "but I haven't been home for ages and I do need new clothes—besides, my sister's getting married." No need to mention that the event was a good six months away; it gave her such a splendid excuse.

They stayed for lunch and Charity tried not to see how charming Everard could be. Dominic was charming too, but he had eyes only for his wife, although his manners were perfect; he looked at her as though she were the sun and moon and stars all rolled into one, thought poor Charity, and when she caught the professor's eye upon her, frowned fiercely at him.

They didn't have much to say to each other on the way back to Utrecht and although she had half expected him to mention her leaving, he said no word about it, but left her at the door of the Home with a hasty excuse that he was due at the hospital for a consultation. She was about to go in when he called after her: "I forgot—my grandmother would like you to have tea with her tomorrow. I shall be away— could you walk round, or would you like Potter to bring the car round?"

Charity stood still, considering. She had nothing to do and as it was Sunday there was no shopping she could invent—besides, he wasn't going to be there. She scowled; escorting the doormat, probably; she still didn't believe his denial of their future marriage.

"Very well," she said at length, and a little ungraciously.

The old lady was resting in her room when Potter admitted her and showed her into the sitting-room, begging her to make herself comfortable until her hostess came down from her room in a few minutes. He also remarked respectfully that he was very glad to see her once more as he poked up the cheerful log fire and went quietly from the room. Left alone, Charity started on a tour of inspection; she viewed a number of portraits of sober and severe-looking gentlemen, presumably the professor's forebears, sat, for purely sentimental reasons, in his chair, and went to pore over the silver in the cabinet. She would take another look at the gemel ring—the ring which would remain there, he had said, until he gave it to the woman he loved.

It wasn't there. She looked at each shelf carefully and then looked again. Only the space where it had rested was clearly to be seen. She went white, picturing it upon the doormat's finger; he would have put it there on that Friday evening when he had told her, quite openly, that he was taking the creature to dine.

Charity went and sat down, feeling shattered. While the ring had been there there had always been hope, however ridiculous that seemed, but now she could stop dreaming her fairy tales. The door opened and she got up to greet Mevrouw van Tijlen, smiling determinedly.

CHAPTER NINE

CHARITY GOT THROUGH her visit with commendable self-control, though perhaps her laugh was a little too frequent and her voice a shade too loud. Her green eyes glittered with the strong feelings bottled up inside her, and when she rose to leave she bade the old lady goodbye in a falsely bright voice, saying that as she would be returning to England within a few days, there might be no opportunity of seeing her before she left.

Her hostess's reply was tart as well as gruff. "Huh—running away, are you?"

"I am not running away," protested Charity with dignity. "There is nothing to run away from."

Mevrouw van Tijlen fumbled among her chains and produced her lorgnette so that she might study Charity the better. Her voice was still tart. "Oh, yes, there is—your future. But perhaps you prefer to spend it in some hospital, ministering to the sick." She sniffed delicately. "Girls aren't what they were."

"I am not chasing after any man." Charity's voice was almost as tart and very determined.

The old lady looked shocked. "I should hope not indeed!" she exclaimed. "That is for the man, in his

own time and in his own way, of course. One needs
patience.'' She went on craftily, ''You remember
what Everard said about the gemel ring, do you not?
It is still in the cabinet, child.''

Charity bent to kiss the soft old cheek. ''No, it's
not,'' she said in a voice devoid of all feeling.
''That's why I'm going back to England.''

She tackled Juffrouw Blom about giving up her job
when she got back and Corrie admitted that she was
quite able to resume her work; she couldn't get
around all that well, but there would be no problem
with stairs, for there was a lift—besides, Mevrouw
Smit would be coming back from her holidays in less
than a week. ''If you would stay just a day or two
longer,'' she begged, ''I know how much you want
to go home.''

''Of course I'll stay,'' Charity assured her; she
didn't want to go home at all, she didn't want to go
anywhere, only stay close to Everard, an impossibility
which she would have to acknowledge finally and the
sooner the better. Old Mevrouw van Tijlen had been
quite right; while the gemel ring had been in its case,
she had clung to the hope that there was still a chance
because he didn't love anyone else.

The doormat must have some hidden attraction,
though heaven knew she had looked insipid enough
at the opera, thought Charity sourly. Probably she
came from an impeccable background—Everard

would make a good husband, she had no doubt, and a splendid father, even to a row of dreary, spectacled children, who would, of course, take after their equally dreary mother... She turned her back on Juffrouw Blom and stared out of the window, seeing nothing because her eyes were full of tears. A clutch of small Everards would have been nice; she remembered Abigail van Wijkelen's and the look on her face when she spoke of her son, and Dominic was besotted with her... She turned back towards the bed into which she had just helped Corrie.

"Will you mention it to the professor?" she asked, "or shall I?"

"I'll say something—I know that he would like me back as soon as possible, he said so. Not," she added hastily, "that he finds you unsatisfactory, Charity, on the contrary he is very pleased with you, he said that too. But there is the buying to do for the month, and the decorators are coming to paint the dining-room." She stopped to think. "I am so very grateful to you, and I know that when Mevrouw Smit gets back, she will be grateful also. It is not perhaps work for a young girl—the excitement of hospital..."

Her remark reminded Charity that she hadn't a job, she hadn't even begun to think about one; she had no idea where she wanted to go either. She made a mental resolve there and then to start looking for one the day she got home. She tried to work up some enthusiasm about her future and failed utterly; she didn't

care what she did, she didn't care if she never saw
the inside of a hospital again. She said suddenly:
"Look, do you mind if I speak to the professor? Perhaps it might look better—I could see him tomorrow,
he'll be along for morning surgery, won't he?"

But as it turned out, she saw him much sooner than
that.

She had been in bed for more than an hour, lying
awake, staring into the dark and listening to the carillons competing with each other every quarter of an
hour, when the intercom buzzed. It was Mevrouw
Laagemaat's quavery voice asking for help. Charity
flung on her dressing-gown, a frivolous garment of
patterned voile with a great many ruffles and a sash,
thrust her feet into a pair of equally frivolous slippers
and tore through the silent corridors and up to the
next floor where the old couple had their flat. The
door was open, Mevrouw Laagemaat was standing
just inside, wringing her hands. Terrified out of her
wits, Charity noted, but unscathed—it would be old
Mijnheer Laagemaat.

He was lying on the bed, apparently asleep. She
could hear his loud uneven breathing as she crossed
the room, and she knew what his pulse would be like
before she lifted his bony, fragile wrist. She knew that
he was deeply unconscious too; even in the dim light
of the old-fashioned silk-shaded lamp, his colour was
shocking. To get the doctor was paramount; stopping
only to beg the old lady to make coffee, because she

would feel better if she had something to do, Charity sped back along the corridor to the telephone and dialled the professor's number.

It was Potter who answered, and when she said: "Potter, please get the professor, it's urgent," was reassured by his quiet: "Right away, miss," and still further reassured by Everard's voice within seconds, asking her what was the matter.

"It's Mijnheer Laagemaat," she said without preamble, and gave him a quick, careful account of him, not wasting a word in the telling, and when he said: "I'll be over in five minutes," she said merely:

"Thank you, Everard," unconscious of the fact that she had called him by name.

She was back with the old man when the professor walked in, looking oddly youthful in slacks and a high-necked sweater, but he had his case with him and when he had finished his quick examination, he wasted no time in opening it and giving her a phial.

"Give that," he told her quietly. "It won't do much good, but it will make things easier for him." He gave her a brief direct look. "There's no chance— an hour or so, perhaps less. Where is his wife?"

"I asked her to make coffee for you—to give her something to do."

"Good girl," his voice was warmly approving. "See to that injection, I'm going to talk to her."

She had done as he had bidden her and tidied the bed when he spoke from the kitchen door. "Come here, Charity—we'll leave Mevrouw Laagemaat with him for a little while, she wants that.''

The two of them stood, side by side in the tiny room, with its old-fashioned gingham frills and geraniums on the sill, and the little oil cooking stove the old lady preferred to the new-fangled electric oven. The coffee was hot and tasted good and they had two cups, saying little, for there was nothing to say. Charity had gone to perch on the table, her extravagant gown billowing around her, her hair tumbling down her back. Her face, without its make-up, looked very young and tired. But she was unaware of this, indeed she had not given her appearance a thought; her mind was centred on the old man.

"Is there anything else I can do? Do you want me to telephone you when he…or shall I wait until the morning?"

He put down his cup. "You won't need to do either, I'll stay. You see, I've known them for a long time. Now I'm going to send Mevrouw Laagemaat here and you see that she has some coffee, will you? and bring her back. We shan't have very long to wait."

The old lady was docile and very calm now. She drank her coffee, insisted on washing up the cups and saucers with Charity's help, and then went back into the bedroom. The old man's breathing had become very quiet now, drowned by the harsh tick-tock of the marble clock on the draped mantelpiece. The professor got up, pushed the old lady gently into a chair by the bed and sat down beside her, while Charity took the little chair he had set ready for her. He began to talk almost at once, in a quite normal voice, and although she couldn't understand anything of what he said, Charity could hear the kindness in his voice. The old lady heard it too, responding to it with a few murmured words and even an occasional smile. And when the old man died, so gently that it was hard to tell, she followed the professor out of the little room, leaving Charity to do the small necessary tasks which needed to be done.

When she joined them presently, Mevrouw Laagemaat was standing with his arms around her, crying into his shoulder. But she didn't cry for long; he sat her down in one of the squat, overstuffed chairs arranged stiffly around the centre table and glanced up at Charity. "This is how she always hoped it would be," he told her, "so although she grieves, she is happy too."

Charity, studying his quiet calm face, stifled an urge to weep herself; for Mevrouw Laagemaat, because she would have to go on alone for a little while longer, after a lifetime of sharing, and in some half-understood way, for herself, because she was alone already and had not yet shared her life with anyone. She gulped back the lump in her throat and said huskily: "I'll make some coffee, shall I? And where shall I put Mevrouw Laagemaat for the night?"

The professor thought briefly. "There's Mevrouw Smit's room next to Bep. Put her in there, then there will be someone close by. You'll have to get Bep up anyway, but get the old lady settled first. I'll give her something to make her sleep."

So it was arranged and presently he took his leave with an abrupt: "Come with me, Charity, and bolt the door after me."

She found herself padding silently beside him through the dim, quiet passages and down the stairs to the side door, his own unhurried tread almost as silent.

At the door he paused. "Go to bed as soon as you can," he counselled her. "I'll be round just after eight, I'll see to everything then." He smiled at her, making nonsense of her resolution to be gone at the first opportunity. "Thank you, Charity. I'm sorry this had to happen while you were here." He put a large hand under her chin and tilted her face up to study it. "You are good and kind and gentle, as well as being clever." He bent his head and kissed her gently. "You are also very beautiful."

Charity did what was necessary with Bep's help. Only when they were finished and Bep had gone back to her bed and she herself was once more in her room did she allow herself to think her own thoughts. It was almost three o'clock; she would have to be up soon after six, she set her alarm clock and climbed tiredly into bed, longing to sort out the night's hap-

penings and too tired to make sense of them. She
would be clearer-headed by morning, she told herself
drowsily, and slept on the thought.

She wasn't clear-headed at all. It was agony to get
up after so short a night's rest. She dressed quickly,
paying little attention to her pale, weary face, bundled
up her hair anyhow, ramming the pins in with a fine
disregard for her appearance, and went downstairs to
the kitchen.

There was coffee on the stove; she felt better when
she had a cup. She put a second cup on a tray and
went upstairs to Juffrouw Blom's room. The inmates
were beginning to stir; she could hear faint elderly
voices, taps running, kettles being filled; soon it
would be time to go round with her little tray of med-
icines. Juffrouw Blom was awake and heaved herself
up against her pillows as she went in. "What happened?" she asked at once. "I can see that you have
had no sleep. Something went wrong—someone was
ill."

Charity poured them each a cup of coffee and
perched on the bed. It was nice to lay the burden of
the night's happenings on to Corrie's broad shoulders.
Juffrouw Blom listened to her tale without interrup-
tion and then nodded her head. "You did well."

"There wasn't much to do," protested Charity.

"No dramatic treatment, no. But who wants that
when they are very old? Comfort and care and a

shoulder to cry on, that is what is needed. The professor would not have it otherwise."

Charity remembered how gentle he had been with the old lady. "No, I know that. He's coming after eight o'clock. Should I get Mevrouw Laagemaat up? I peeped in just now and she's still sleeping."

"Leave her. Professor van Tijlen will do all that is necessary, as he always does, but have some coffee ready for him—it is his theatre day and he will go straight there without his breakfast if we do not prevent him."

"But he can't do that," protested Charity. "Someone ought to see that he has something—his lists are so long."

Juffrouw Blom's glance flickered over her and away again. "That is what I think also. A good wife, that is what he needs." She drank the rest of her coffee, and when she spoke again it was about something quite different, but when Charity got up to go she asked: "You're sure you want to tell him about going? I could do it later on—he is sure to come in this evening, or even tomorrow."

"No, I think I'd rather do it, Corrie. There are only Mevrouw Kist and Mijnheer Jasper on the list for surgery so far, and neither of them will take long."

She hurried off to the kitchen again, forming sentences in her head—polite phrases about how much she had enjoyed her work and how much she wanted to go home, for she had made up her mind while she had been with Corrie that she wouldn't let last night alter her purpose; he would have been grateful to anyone in similar circumstances. His kiss had been kind, the sort of kiss one would give a tired old lady or an unhappy child. She realised that she had a headache and that her temper was uncertain; she would have a nap after lunch and take a couple of Panadol straight away, but one thing and another hindered her from fetching them, and she still hadn't taken them when the slight creak of the side door heralded the professor.

She should have been delighted to see him, but somehow the sight of him, looking as though he had had a long restful night's sleep, immaculately dressed as he always was, his face placid, set her nerves on edge. His cheerful greeting did nothing to improve this feeling; she muttered briefly and asked: "Shall I fetch you some coffee now or would you prefer it later on? And do you want to take the surgery first?"

He appeared not to notice her moroseness but stood relaxed, smiling down at her. "You haven't had enough sleep," he told her. "My poor girl, you're as cross as two sticks, aren't you?" He walked to the desk. "I'll do the form-filling and so forth and some telephoning and have my coffee while I do it, if I may. I shall want you here to check times and so forth," he finished, vaguely.

Charity fetched his coffee and a plate of buttered toast besides, and then, because he refused to have anything unless she had a cup herself, went back to the kitchen again for another lot of coffee. Their drinks poured, she perched silently on a chair beside the desk and watched him as he wrote until presently he cast down his pen and glanced at her.

"So—that is settled." He bit into his toast, drank some of the coffee and pulled the telephone towards him. His calls made, he sat back, munching toast while he gave her a brief outline of what had been arranged. This done, he suggested that he should see the surgery patients.

"There are only two," explained Charity. "Mevrouw Kist has a sore mouth and Mijnheer Jasper has a nasty little cough." She got up to precede him to the door. "It seems so funny," she mused aloud, "that you should be so deeply interested in old people..."

"Ah, you mean that my interest should be centred upon the operating table and not upon the actual person. But there, dear girl, you are at fault, I am deeply interested in people—more than you might suppose." He shot her a sidelong glance full of amusement. "You would wish me to become a dry as dust surgeon who thinks only of his work. I admit my work is very important to me, although just lately I have to realise that there are other things equally important. No, Charity, when I am out of theatre, my mind is filled with only the pleasantest of thoughts."

Against her better judgment, she asked: "What thoughts?"

They were in the gloomy hall, not hurrying. "You, for instance," he said.

She said sharply: "Not me—Juffrouw van Stassen."

He halted his leisurely progress. "Now why do you say that? I believe that I gave you my reasons for not pursuing my intentions in that quarter."

"You were joking." Charity was feeling crosser and crosser with every minute which passed. "You didn't really expect me to believe you? Just because I was rude about her wouldn't be a reason for not seeing her again—and you did—you took her to dinner..."

He was eyeing her with the greatest interest. "Am I to understand from your dreadful muddled remarks that you mind my seeing her again?"

"You don't have to understand anything," said Charity recklessly. Her head was really very bad, she hardly knew what she was saying, although she suspected that presently, when she could think clearly again, she would bitterly regret most of what she was saying now. They had reached the surgery door; without giving him an opportunity to say more, she opened it and ushered him in.

His two patients were soon dealt with. Charity saw them on their elderly way and went back to clear up the few things the professor had used. She was washing her hands at the sink while he tidied away their notes when he said to surprise her: "Something is on your mind, Charity, and it's not just a headache, is it?"

He had unwittingly forced her hand; there was nothing for it but to tell him that she would like to leave. She did it in a rambling way, getting to the point only after a great many explanations and excuses, and so intent on making the whole thing sound perfectly normal that she didn't notice the expression on his face. At length he cut through her breathless, repetitive chatter.

"Why do you want to leave?" he asked flatly. "Oh, I know you want to go home, you have told me that several times in as many minutes, but what is the real reason?"

She took refuge in a haughty coldness. "There is no reason."

He gave her a mocking smile. "Juffrouw van Stassen, perhaps?" he asked her blandly.

She flared up at that; words which she hardly knew she was uttering went tumbling off her tongue at a fine rate. "I'm sick of her!" she told him; a shade too loudly. "I don't care if you marry her—she'll be a h-horrid wife, but of course you won't care, you're so besotted..."

He was sitting on the side of the desk, swinging a leg, looking remarkably composed. "Besotted?" He looked thoughtfully at her. "You know, I can only

recall one occasion when you saw Juffrouw van Stassen and myself together—in public, if you remember,
and I pride myself on containing my deeper feelings
in public.''

"Oh, don't be so pompous!" Her green eyes
flashed at him, she was in a fine temper by now.
"And I don't believe you have any deeper feelings."
She hiccoughed with choked rage and tears. "Of
course you're besotted—you gave her the gemel ring,
I know you did, it isn't in the cabinet any more."

His expression had not altered at this remarkable
speech, only his eyes gleamed beneath their lids. All
he said was: "Neither is it. I had no idea that you
were so interested in its history." His raised eyebrows, invited her to continue.

"I'm not—I couldn't c-care less, only your grandmother told me, and I just happened to notice." She
flew off at a sudden tangent. "I can't think why I
ever agreed to come here and work for you..."

"Nor can I, Charity. I was beginning to think that
I had the answer, but perhaps I was wrong."

She snapped: "Well, you have to be wrong, sometimes," and turned her back on him because if she
looked at him for a moment longer she would burst
into tears. "When will it be convenient for me to
go?" she asked him in a low voice.

"Whenever you wish." His voice was very even.
"Charity, do you want to go?"

Pride made her say: "Of course I do."

"We would not see each other again." His voice was mild enough.

It was shocking, but she was unable to prevent one dreadful lie piling up on the next. "I don't care—I don't want to see you again."

She had controlled her voice at last; it was cold and quiet and in her own ears it sounded convincing; it must have sounded convincing to the professor too, for he got down off the desk, saying without heat:

"That settles the question, doesn't it? I shall be away for a few days, arrange something with Corrie, will you—I'll send your cheque."

He started for the door, and Charity stood at the sink, drying her hands again, trying to think of something she could say to stop him, short of telling him that she loved him and life was never going to be the same again.

She wasn't really listening when he said: "I am grateful to you for all your help, Charity. You have been more than generous with your time and services—I do not know what we should have done without you, and I never heard you grumble."

He retraced his steps and stood in front of her. "It is useless to say that we part as friends—all the same, I wish you well, dear girl." He smiled at her, a smile of such kindliness that she actually had her mouth open to tell him that she didn't want to leave him, ever—but no sound came; when she finally achieved a whispered "Everard," he had gone.

* * *

There was nothing left to do but explain as best she could to Corrie, decide which day to leave, and book a seat on a flight from Schiphol.

Corrie was upset at the idea of losing her, but she made no fuss, for she had been expecting her to leave within the next week. She was up and walking with a stick now and declared quite cheerfully that she could manage very well until Mevrouw Smit returned, so Charity booked her flight for the day after next, telephoned her mother and plunged once more into the day's routine, her ears stretched for the telephone, the door, the postman or the sound of the Lamborghini's gentle snort, but although the telephone rang times out of number, as did the front door bell, not to mention the postman delivering a sizeable mail, there was nothing for her. She even stayed up late, sitting in the office until midnight, hoping that perhaps Everard would come, although her common sense told her that there was absolutely no reason why he should. She went to bed finally, and spent a miserable night.

The next day dragged intolerably; Charity flung herself into the business of checking the laundry—no mean task—made up beds, helped the more frail to take their baths, ran errands for Juffrouw Blom, who had wedged herself into the office once more and more or less assumed command and even then found herself after the midday meal with time on her hands. The temptation to visit Mevrouw van Tijlen was very great, but she resisted it and went resolutely to the shops, where she bought more presents for her family and a glamorous nightie for Corrie. Somehow the evening crept by; before she went to bed she telephoned the professor's house and when Potter answered asked him to give his mistress her love and tell her that she was leaving in the morning, and gained a morsel of comfort from his sincere ''I'm sorry to hear that, Miss Dawson, indeed I am, me and Mrs Potter, both.''

She thanked him, bade him goodbye and hung up, reflecting that she had met a number of very pleasant people while she had been in Holland; it was a pity that she was unlikely to see them again.

She spent another sleepless night, and in the morning she left.

Home looked just the same. It was autumn now, of course, and the garden was full of dahlias and chrysanthemums and late roses. The virginia creeper which rioted over the house was turning colour, presenting a welcoming and well-remembered picture. There was no doubt that her family were glad to see her again, although they were not unduly curious as to what she had been doing, probably because Lucy's wedding, although still some six months away, took the lion's share of their attention. She was to have a big wedding, for the Colonel and his wife were well known in Budleigh Salterton and had a great number of friends. Both Charity's parents and her sister took it for granted that she would be there for the wedding.

"You must get something close by," advised her mother, "so that there will be no difficulty about travelling and time off. I don't suppose that nice professor wants you back again? I do hope not, for there will be your dress to fit and the flowers and..."

"The wedding isn't for six months," Charity reminded her parent patiently. "I thought I'd have a week at home now and start looking around for something."

She had been home for exactly two days when Potter telephoned. His voice sounded clear in her ears, as respectful as he always had been, only now there was an undercurrent of something else she couldn't define.

"Miss Dawson? I'm relieved to find you at your home. It's Mevrouw van Tijlen—she's not at all well and she asked me to telephone you. She would like you to come and stay with her, just for a few days. She is, I think, a little nervous."

"Is the professor not home?" asked Charity with unnatural calm.

"No, miss—he went to Vienna, and Mevrouw won't allow me to telephone him because he's attending some important conference there. I'm a little worried, miss."

"Potter, I'm only just home."

"I understand, miss. Only I had hoped—however, I'll let Mevrouw know."

It was too much; the old lady was Everard's grandmother and he loved her, and so, in a way, Charity loved her too—and she might be very ill, she was old as well; she knew that she would never forgive herself if anything happened to the old lady while Everard was away.

"All right, Potter. I'll come. I'll get a flight some time today if I can."

"I'm very relieved, miss." He sounded it too. "If you would be good enough to telephone when you know the time of your flight, I'll meet you at Schiphol with the Daimler, miss."

"Thank you, Potter, I'll ring you back."

Charity went in search of her mother, who heard her out and said finally:

"Well, darling, it's wretched for you—just as you've got home, too, but I can quite understand how you feel about it." She shot her elder daughter a shrewd look. "I'm sure your father will agree with you. Do you want any help with packing?"

It was surprising how quickly Charity flung a few things into a small case while her father telephoned London Airport. It was still only mid-morning when her father drove her into Exeter to catch the London express; by late afternoon she was at Schiphol.

Summer had left Holland; the sky was overcast and of a uniform grey and there was a chilly wind; Charity was glad of her green tweed suit and thin woolly sweater as she made her way to the airport's entrance.

Potter was waiting, his manner nicely welcoming. Mevrouw van Tijlen, he told her as they drove towards Utrecht, was better, the doctor had told her to rest more. Charity, putting searching questions, received vague answers which she put down to lack of knowledge on Potter's part; Mevrouw van Tijlen, as he pointed out, was well into her eighties, and far too active.

"She has always taken such an interest in the professor's work, miss—very proud of him, she is, wouldn't hinder him for the world. Most devoted they are—it's a close knit family, as you might say, even though there's only cousins and aunts and uncles and such like."

"I should have thought that Mevrouw van Tijlen would have preferred a member of the family to be with her," hazarded Charity.

She didn't notice his pause. "Well, miss, they're scattered around as you might say, and I think that Mevrouw is afraid that if I get in touch with one of them, they would let the professor know, and that's something she won't hear of."

"Well, I can understand that, Potter. Just so long as she's not seriously ill—but you say that she isn't— let's hope she will be well again by the time Professor van Tijlen gets back. When will that be?"

Potter became vague again. "That's a thing I can't say, miss. Mevrouw will know."

Charity stared out at the quiet countryside. It would be dusk soon; there were already lights in some of the houses. She would have to explain to Mevrouw van Tijlen that she intended to leave before the professor returned—nothing, absolutely nothing, would induce her to see him again. Let bygones be bygones. She elaborated this with: "Least said, soonest mended," adding for good measure: "Don't cry over spilt milk". None of these sensible sayings gave her the least comfort. She wrenched her thoughts back to the present. "You're a first-rate driver, Potter," she told her companion.

He glowed gently. "Thank you, miss. I've been at it for years, you might say—drove a tank at the end of the last war."

"Now that is interesting," observed Charity, and being her father's daughter, plunged into the subject with intelligent enthusiasm. "Tell me about it."

They were still deeply engrossed when they reached the professor's house, where they were admitted by Mrs Potter, breathing a welcome in both Dutch and English. She led the way upstairs without loss of time, while Potter, coming behind them with Charity's case, explained that Mevrouw van Tijlen had asked if she would go and see her as soon as she had settled in.

But first Charity was to dine, interposed Mrs Potter,

in half an hour in the dining room, if that pleased Miss Dawson, and Charity, healthily hungry, agreed that half an hour would suit her very nicely as she followed the housekeeper down an arched passage on the first floor, leading to the back of the house. It surprised her that the house was so large, for they seemed to be passing door after door. It was Potter who saw her glancing around her and who volunteered the information that the house went a long way back from the street. "There's a nice bit of garden, too, miss," he volunteered.

Charity inspected the garden presently, after they had left her in a room with two long, wide windows overlooking one of the prettiest bits of garden she had ever set eyes on. True it was small, but planned so delightfully that there was room for several white-painted wrought iron chairs and a small table, a little walnut tree to shade them, and a banked-up flower bed against its end wall. The small slip of lawn was very green and upon it rested a round basket, in which she could see a tabby cat with three kittens. As she looked, straining her eyes a little because dusk was rapidly turning to the evening's dark, a door opened somewhere below and Mrs Potter appeared, to scoop up the basket and its contents and bear it indoors, a homely gesture which somehow made the day's happenings seem quite normal.

She turned away from the evening outside and gave her attention to the room. It was large and high-

ceilinged and furnished to perfection with a little can-
opied bed, a Hepplewhite dressing-table and a small
davenport against one wall. The furnishings were pale
pastels whose delicate tones were echoed in the ad-
joining bathroom, and if that were not enough, there
were several small, extremely comfortable chairs arranged invitingly with reading tables handy, each with
its tinted lamp and pile of books and magazines. Very
luxurious, thought Charity, exploring, and wondered
what Everard would say if he knew that she was here,
in his house.

She did her hair and her face and went back along
the passage and down the stairs, where she found Potter waiting in the hall, ready to usher her into the
dining-room, to sit solitary at a great oval table, with
its heavy candlesticks and flower centrepiece. She
drank her soup slowly, looking around her as she did
so. Here was more evidence of the professor's wealth;
she had never quite believed in it, but now she had
proof of it and found it a little daunting—the table
silver she was using was old and genuine, as were the
delicate porcelain plates from which she ate her delicious dinner. She was glad when the meal was over
and she could go to Mevrouw van Tijlen.

The old lady was in bed, perched up against a number of pillows, frilled and embroidered, their square
vastness making her look very small, but not, Charity
was quick to observe, in the least ill.

"Dear child," said Mevrouw van Tijlen, "how

good of you to come, and how tiresome an old woman can become—but after Everard had gone I felt so peculiar. I know it is only my age and silly nerves, but I made myself quite ill, and when Dr de Wal came to see me and I told him about you, he thought it a splendid idea for you to come and keep me company while I am alone.''

Charity listened quietly to the gruff little voice. Of course the old lady wasn't alone; the Potters were devoted to her and she had herself seen two maids in the house as well; she would have to make it quite clear about leaving before Everard returned and discovered her.

''I'm glad to see you're not too poorly,'' she said warmly, ''and of course I didn't mind coming—I wasn't doing anything at home. But there is one thing. I don't want to be here when the professor returns. I shall want to leave before that. Can that be arranged, do you think?''

Mevrouw van Tijlen's answer wasn't very direct. ''Well, he's been gone, let me see, two days—one of those meetings, you know, in Vienna—a lovely city, I went there as a girl. They last a very long time, but whenever he is away, he telephones me the day before he returns, so that will give you plenty of time to pack your things and go, my dear.'' She stared at Charity. ''You're quite sure you don't want to meet him?''

''Yes, quite sure.''

The little figure in the vast bed wriggled and fidgeted and Charity went to rearrange the pillows.

"I was under the impression that you loved Everard."

There seemed no point in pretending. "I do, you know that."

Mevrouw van Tijlen's eyes sparkled. She looked at the little silver clock on the bedside table and said suddenly: "Sit down, child, and tell me about your home—that is if you are not too tired."

Charity sat, denying tiredness. "But is there nothing I can do for you? I had thought that you were in need of a nurse…"

Her companion waved a bony hand. "Not tonight, Charity, but I would enjoy a chat. I have been worried, but now that you are here, I feel better already."

So Charity talked; about her home and the country around it and Lucy's wedding. Mevrouw van Tijlen was deep in a description of her own wedding dress when she interrupted herself somewhat abruptly:

"Dear child, will you go downstairs to Everard's study and fetch my spectacles? How foolish of me to have forgotten to ask Potter to bring them up—I need them in the night, you know—if I can't sleep."

Charity jumped to her feet at once, glad to be of some use, however slight. "Of course, where are they exactly? And won't the professor mind me going to his study?"

The old lady peeped at her from under her brows.

"He won't mind—look in the second drawer on the left of his desk. The drawers are locked, but the keys are kept in the centre drawer." She glanced again at the clock. "Will you go now, my dear, before we start talking again and forget?"

Charity went, reflecting that the old were sometimes possessed of a quite irrational impatience. There was no one about downstairs, the hall was softly lighted, the study door, behind the dining-room, was shut. She opened it and went inside.

It was, as were most of the rooms in the house, large and lofty, and in this case, austere. Books lined the walls, the desk in its centre was large and laden with the impedimenta she had come to accept as a necessity for most members of the medical profession; journals, samples, patients' notes, memo pads and two telephones, all jostling for a place. There was a big chair behind the desk.

She put her hand lovingly upon it for a moment and then turned to the centre drawer to find the keys. She had just fitted one into the second drawer on the left when the professor came in.

Charity's surprise was so profound that she was speechless, all she could do was to stare, her pretty mouth open. But surprise had no such effect upon the professor; he spoke with obvious wrath, something explosive in his own tongue before recovering his usual calm manner as he advanced towards her without haste. "My dear girl," he said blandly, "so this is the urgent matter for which Grandmother demanded my return.''

He put out a hand and took the bunch of keys from her nerveless fingers, laid them on the desk and whisked her into his arms, to kiss her with deep satisfaction and at some length, and Charity, after the faintest of protests, kissed him back.

Presently, though, she found her tongue, although her voice was annoyingly squeaky with the strength of her feelings. ''But you aren't expected back—you went away for some time—you weren't to be worried…''

He sorted out these fragments of information. ''But I am back—who told you I wasn't expected, my darling girl?—and I do wonder why you are here.''

She thought about being called his darling girl before she replied: ''Potter, that is, your grandmother said…''

He smiled suddenly. ''Sufficiently good reason for you to rifle my desk?''

She flared up. ''I was not rifling your desk! I was fetching your grandmother's spectacles—they're in the second drawer on the left—she told me to look there.''

She saw his eyes light up with laughter. ''And Grandmother—and Potter—told you that I wouldn't be back?'' He kissed her again with satisfying thoroughness. ''Potter would say anything Grandmother told him to—she winds him round her little finger, she winds me round her little finger too, but you, my dearest darling, you wind me round your heart, we fit together, like the gemel ring. Grandmother, being old and impatient, has been anticipating fate, for of course, fate would have brought us together again.''

"You mean that your grandmother isn't ill at all? She didn't want a nurse—she arranged it all?''

"Yes, my darling.''

She persisted, following a train of thought. "But supposing I had refused to come, or you hadn't come back, or...''

"Grandmother, I'm afraid to say, is a bit of a gambler.''

There was a great deal not clear to her. She pulled away from his arms and was at once caught and held more firmly than before. When he spoke his voice was quiet and tender. "Do you know, my darling, that I never realised that I loved you? not until the other day in the Home when you accused me of preventing you from going back to England. And it was true, only all that time I never really knew, despite the fact that I looked for you everywhere I went, and made excuses to visit Mr Boekerchek—and when I found you all on your own during the fire, I wanted to pick you up and rush you to safety, and each time something kept you from returning to England I was happy. I came back here that day and took the gemel ring and put it here, in this drawer, with some half-formed plan in my head that I would bring you here and give it to you—only you were so fierce with me, saying that you wanted to go away. And I let you go, knowing very well that I would follow you because I wouldn't be able to help myself.''

He loosed her at last and opened the drawer and drew out the little red box and took the gemel ring from it and put it on her finger. ''We'll marry, my dear love? and soon?''

''Yes, Everard.'' Her eyes glowed greenly as she smiled up at him with a hint of mischief. ''But perhaps I should warn you that I'm not a doormat.''

''And thank God for it, my love, for I suspect that between us we shall produce a bunch of healthy, naughty children—though I think we should content ourselves with rather less than the dozens you wished on me.''

''With no glasses?'' asked Charity, and reached up to kiss him.

''No glasses,'' promised the professor.

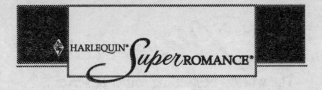
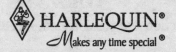

HARLEQUIN® *Presents*

The world's bestselling romance series...
The series that brings you your favorite authors,
month after month:

Helen Bianchin...Emma Darcy
Lynne Graham...Penny Jordan
Miranda Lee...Sandra Marton
Anne Mather...Carole Mortimer
Susan Napier...Michelle Reid

and many more uniquely talented authors!

Wealthy, powerful, gorgeous men...
Women who have feelings just like your own...
The stories you love, set in exotic, glamorous locations...

HARLEQUIN® *Presents*

Seduction and passion guaranteed!

HARLEQUIN®
INTRIGUE

WE'LL LEAVE YOU BREATHLESS!

If you've been looking for thrilling tales of
contemporary passion and sensuous love stories
with taut, edge-of-the-seat suspense—then
you'll love Harlequin Intrigue!

Every month, you'll meet four new heroes
who are guaranteed to make your spine tingle
and your pulse pound. With them you'll enter
into the exciting world of Harlequin Intrigue—
where your life is on the line
and so is your heart!

THAT'S INTRIGUE—
ROMANTIC SUSPENSE
AT ITS BEST!

HARLEQUIN®
Makes any time special ®

Harlequin® Historical

From rugged lawmen and valiant knights to defiant heiresses and spirited frontierswomen, Harlequin Historicals will capture your imagination with their dramatic scope, passion and adventure.

*Harlequin Historicals...
they're too good to miss!*